Blurb

Death. *Loyalty. Love.*

A shadow on the wall, a hooded figure under the moon, a contract to be filled...

Raised as an assassin from birth, Ionia has been given the most dangerous contract yet: to kill the Crown Prince. Only the risk isn't just in losing her life if she fails, but in losing her heart.

When the job goes wrong, and Ionia spares the Prince's life instead of taking it, she's thrust into a tangled web of betrayal, danger, and lies.

Now she has to team up with the same man she tried to kill in order to save not only him, but his friends as well.

In this world of secrets and magic, she'll need to learn to trust her heart, even if it goes against everything she's ever known.

Even if it means her death.

To Save a Prince

Prince

The Kingmaker Chronicles

Indra Frost

Copyright

PLEASE DO NOT SUPPORT PIRACY.

THESE STORIES YOU ENJOY ARE THE RESULT OF
MONTHS OR YEARS OF WORK... SO ARE THE ONES YOU
DON'T ENJOY.

To all the assassins that fell in love with your marks...I feel you.

CHAPTER ONE

I SAT, PERCHED ON THE WALL OUTSIDE the castle's grounds, the moon shining brightly as it mocked me from its place in the sky. It had been a few days since I'd been back here, and I wasn't looking forward to finishing this job. My feelings of doubt about my target weren't helping, either. It wasn't my place to say who did or didn't deserve death, but every time I got close to the Crown Prince, the same uncertain feeling fell over me. It only got worse when his advisor and guard were with him.

I had hesitated last time, not taking the shot when I had it. And it had cost me my first and only chance to take his life. Until tonight.

As I went over my plan one more time, I noticed three hooded figures crossing through a side door of the castle. A combination of instinct and magic told me it was my mark and his associates, and all my well laid plans went to hell in an instant.

I wanted to grumble and curse about lost opportunities, but that wouldn't do any good now. There was also a part of me that was relieved by the change of plans, and that was the part of me that I would need to beat into submission later. I would work out my body to the point of utter exhaustion, and then I would push myself to go even further. Maybe, if I couldn't move or think, I would get it into my head that it wasn't my *job* to think. It was my job to *obey*.

The three hooded men made it across the distance to the far wall unnoticed by the guards, and with the number of armored solders wandering around, it let me know that one of the three was using a cloaking spell to accomplish the feat. If that were the case, it would make my job more difficult. But not impossible. I wasn't exactly lacking in the magic department myself, and so far, there hadn't been a spell that had been able to fool me.

Debating over what to do, I decided to follow the three men, who I was now going to call the Idiot Brigade, and see what they were up to. Maybe seeing what they were about to do would help me find my resolve to complete this job.

My own cloaking spell in place, I stood and ran along the large stone structure on silent feet towards where I had seen them climb over to the other side. Jumping, I landed with a rolling movement before I started to run after them. As soon as they were in my sights, I slowed down and kept my distance, tracking and watching them without giving away my position.

The moon was glowing brightly, and caution had me staying back further than was probably necessary with my own cloaking spell in place. No one had been able to see through it before, but that didn't mean it was impossible. I could see through the three men's in front of me, so it never hurt to be prepared.

The night air was cool as I watched the Idiot Brigade with frustrated amusement. They were joking quietly, ribbing each other as they made their way towards one of the poorer towns in the kingdom that was within walking distance. The trees stood tall over our heads, and yet, with the three men together, they almost seemed to feel smaller somehow.

Confusion ran through me when I realized exactly where they were headed. What did a Crown Prince need in that area? Sure, some of the best tradesmen were in these poorer towns, but they didn't have the titles or following that the others in the better cities did. The tradesmen I was sure someone of royal birth would be more accustomed to working with.

As the small town came into view, the Idiot Brigade continued to walk along the tree line while still wearing their cloaks.

I couldn't deny that I was curious about their reasons for coming to this small district. This wasn't the first time I had seen the three men run off into the night, but it *was* the first time I had followed them. And all it had done was add more confusion to the mix of emotions running through me.

Curiosity had killed the cat, but seeing him and his friends put the effort into sneaking here in the middle of the night had done nothing but make me more curious. An emotion that would get me into trouble.

All I could do was hope that the Prince and his friends were here for some nefarious purpose, and that my conscience would be appeased when I killed him later that night.

That damn Prince just had to go and be a nice guy.

I cursed silently to myself as I followed them back to the castle. I had been so ready to condemn him for his actions, for his supposed crimes, but it turned out that he had been there to *help*. Who's ever heard of a Crown Prince getting his hands dirty to help the poor people of his kingdom?

Not me, not before now. And now it would be impossible for

me to kill him.

Frustration flowed through me as I followed them back towards the castle. The sun threating to rise above the mountain peaks with every step closer to the looming building. The Prince had been gone longer than usual tonight, helping one of the shopkeepers start to rebuild his shop after a fire had nearly burned it to the ground.

I didn't know who I was more disgusted with, him, or myself. I shivered as I thought of going back to the guild empty-handed. There would be a severe punishment for my failure, and what was worse, they would just send someone else to finish the job.

All my denial to finish the job would do was delay his death, not stop it.

Something in my chest shriveled at my own thoughts. I wasn't a good person, not like the men before me. I was raised from a young age to take lives, not save them, and I was good at it. One of the best. The Guild Master wasn't generous to those who failed, and I hadn't enjoyed being at the center of his attention, so I had made it my goal to be good at what I did, and to get there fast.

Not that I had much choice with him in charge.

There were some things that the Guild Master knew I wouldn't do, and until now he had respected my wishes. My attempt at having morals was something that I knew the others sneered at me for. But I had proven myself twice over, and none of them could deny that I was good at what I did.

I wouldn't kill children, and I wouldn't take the life of someone who I didn't think deserved it. Though that last rule was looser. There was a lot that I wouldn't stand for, and some offenses were worse than others.

But the Guild Master had *lied* to me this time. This Prince wasn't the monster he had painted him out to be, and as a result, I knew this would be my first failed mission. I *always* observed my marks before I took their lives, he knew that, so why did he send me after someone so utterly *good*?

Another thought came to mind, but it flew out just as quick. He wouldn't have sent me out *wanting* me to fail, would he? It made sense in a twisted sort of way. He didn't like my morals, but he hadn't exactly fought me on them. Until now.

That thought continued to float through my mind as I watched the Idiot Brigade climb the wall outside the palace grounds. Then I used my own strength to jump to the top of the ten-foot stone structure with ease.

Crouching, I rested my head in my hand as I watched my mark make his way back into the castle with his friends. Completely unscathed.

There had been plenty of opportunities tonight to take his life and make it seem like an accident. But I hadn't, and now it would be my price to pay when I went back after failing. My chest squeezed, knowing that they would send someone else to take his life. Someone who wouldn't care that he was a kind and giving man. Someone that would enjoy the kill, and the gold that came with it.

I hesitated, watching the castle doors close behind the three hooded figures. Then sighed, knowing that I couldn't stand by and watch as he fell into the clutches of men who were cold and money hungry.

If nothing else, I had to warn him before I left.

It had been a long time since I had witnessed someone do something for others that wasn't for their own personal gain. And there was a small part of me that wanted to help that kindness thrive. Especially in a world that I only ever saw the dark parts of.

There was no guarantee that I would survive a failure of this magnitude, but I didn't have any choice but to go back. There was nowhere else for me to go. I would just have to hope that the Guild Master was kind enough not to kill me, and instead just gave me a beating to remember. This was my first transgression, even if it was a failure that was bigger than most.

He wouldn't find out about the warning I was going to deliver; that would be a guaranteed death sentence. And yet, I couldn't walk away from this situation without doing something. Even if it did result in my death. What was one less murderer in the world if it saved a genuinely good person?

Decision made, I sat on the wall with my feet dangling over the side to wait. I would visit the Prince the following night. And in the meantime, I would wait and watch him. These humans were curious creatures, after all, and I loved to see what they did with their lives.

Night fell swiftly, with no sign of the Prince or his companions, the moon still shining brightly as she laughed at me.

I stood for the first time since settling down the night before, knowing that this was the best time to make my move if I wanted to catch the Prince alone in his chambers. If I waited too long, there was always a chance I might miss him before he left for his nightly excursion.

With the building that they had helped to patch up still needing work, I had a feeling he would be venturing out again tonight to help the shopkeeper.

Jumping from the wall with silent ease, I calmly walked

across the grounds. Acting like I knew what I was doing and walking with confidence would stop the most curious people. That was if they were able to see through my spell in the first place. But I had done this same walk many nights before and that hadn't happened yet, so I was pretty sure it would hold.

Coming up to the side of the building, I forwent any doors and started to scale the wall. The bricks were nicely spaced, and even without the help of magic it was easy to climb. It didn't take long for me to get to the second floor, and I snuck into one of the empty rooms through the balcony window I had left open on one of my first visits.

All of my senses were alert as I made it to the door, pressing my ear against it as I listened for any sounds that weren't expected. The rustle of clothing was all that I heard, and even those sounded far enough away that I felt safe to leave the room. Opening the door, I peered out, just to make sure that I really was okay. It never hurt to be careful. Nothing seemed off, so I squeezed out, and softly shut the door behind me before moving down the hallway pressed against the wall.

A shadow moved further down the hall and I froze. The cloaking spell around me was in place, but the constantly shifting environment inside a building made it harder to keep up. I didn't want to chance becoming visible by continuing on when I knew someone was coming towards me.

The shadow of a man seemed to get larger as it grew closer, and when he was close enough that I could see his face I realized that I recognized him. He was the Head Knight, and one of the Idiot Brigade that I had followed around the night before.

He made an odd face as he got closer, and I realized with a start that he was probably sensing my presence. Even if the way his brow furrowed indicated that he wasn't quite sure what it was that he was sensing exactly.

That was curious. I hadn't ever met anyone that could sense

me when I was cloaking. Then again, I tended to avoid others whenever possible. I wasn't a very social person; most assassins didn't tend to be when someone was always waiting to stab them in the back.

He sent a suspicious look around, but when he didn't see anything out of place he continued on his way. But I knew, even with this reprieve, that my time was more limited than before. He would figure out what he had sensed in just a moment, and then he would raise the alarm. He was around magic often if the cloaking spell last night was evidence, and he would be able to sense the after effects of my spell once he was out of its range. I had to be gone long before then, or I would be forced to do something I didn't want to in order to escape.

As soon as he was far enough past me, I started to move towards my destination going faster than before. There wasn't time for finesse if I wanted to warn the Prince before I had to leave. And my conscience, along with that stupid lump of muscle in my chest, wouldn't allow me to do anything less.

I pulled my magic closer, hoping to make up for a bit of lost time with my speed. And I didn't slow down, even when I heard the knight make a strangled noise behind me. I peeked back at him as I rounded the corner to find him looking over the area I had been standing moments ago, but he hadn't spotted *me*. So, I continued on with my new self-given mission.

I would warn the Prince, then I would make sure I had done everything else that I needed to before leaving to go back to the guild.

And my possible execution.

I made it to the door of the Prince's rooms without any other close calls, but I was more nervous about the lack of trouble than if I had found some. The alarm hadn't been sounded, yet I knew that my presence had been sensed. It put me on edge and left me to wonder what was about to happen.

There was no way that I was leaving unscathed, but I hoped that I wouldn't need to hurt anyone too badly to get out of here.

Pausing outside his door, I debated on what to say. But then I realized that it didn't really matter what words I spoke. He wasn't going to believe me anyway, not really. But my coming in the first place would plant the seed of doubt in his mind. It would also ensure that all three members of the Idiot Brigade would be more on guard based on the fact that I had managed to get so close to the Prince. I didn't need him to believe my words, just my actions.

Opening the door, I walked into his quarters without pause and headed to his bed chamber. Based on the energy in the room, I knew that was where he currently was. Magic was a powerful force, even more so when I used it to pinpoint the location of a target and attached a spell to them. My target wouldn't be able to shake the spell until I decided that they could. It was a taxing spell to cast, but one that was worth it to make sure that I didn't lose a mark. If they managed to run in the first place.

"I told you that I would meet you near the door in a few minutes, Xavier. There's no need to hover like a worried mother hen," an amused voice called as I moved closer to his room.

"And I'm sure he'll be waiting there for you, just as you told him to," I answered, disguising my voice so that I didn't sound like I normally did as I walked into his room.

But upon entering the room, all the other words that I wanted to say dried up in my mouth. I was left staring at the Prince from under my hood, my eyes wide.

He was a beautiful specimen of a man. His body muscular and toned in a way that showed he was used to hard work and didn't mind getting his hands dirty. Scars littered his body, blade marks and other scars showing that he wasn't afraid of getting hurt, and that he had learned to hone his skills through trial and error. It was a shame that someone so handsome had a price on their head.

His head jerked up to look at me when he heard a voice that he wasn't expecting, and the fast movement was enough to bring me back to the mission at hand. That pause upon entering his room was the first time I had ever lost sight of what I was doing. I had lowered my cloaking spell as I entered his chambers so that I could deliver my warning, but something about the Prince's gaze made me think that having it in place wouldn't have changed a thing. His eyes were intense, searching, as he looked my slight form over, and I did the same to him once more.

I had known the Prince was attractive, but there was a difference between seeing an attractive face from far away and seeing his body, naked and up close and personal.

"Who are you?" He asked, rather calmly considering his initial surprise.

"I've come to warn you that there's a price on your head," I said, ignoring his question.

Something in his gaze shifted, and I grew more wary than before. I wasn't sure what I had just seen, but something told me the Prince held a power all his own, and it may just be a match for mine.

"Are *you* here to kill me?" he asked with a blank face.

He was still naked, standing confidently as his clothes sat beside him, forgotten.

I hesitated in the doorway, surprised that he hadn't called out to the guards as soon as he had seen me. It gave me pause, and I had to reach out to make sure that I still had the other spells around me. This situation was much odder than I had anticipated, and I needed to get out of here as soon as possible. Something wasn't right with these men, and even if I knew that they were good people, I had invaded his space with the intent to kill him at one time. There was no guarantee that he would treat me with any more leeway than the Guild Master would.

"Not anymore," I said, choosing to be honest and watching as his eyes crease with confusion. "But I came to warn you that someone else *will*."

He nodded, but stayed silent, his eyes turning with all the thoughts running through his head.

The sound of bells and alarms rang through the air, and my head jerked toward the hall where I could hear the sound of feet heading our way. I turned my head back to warn the Prince one last time, only to find that he was less than a foot away from me.

I jerked back, not having expected to have him so close to me. He moved just as silently as I did, but I should have sensed him getting closer regardless of how quietly he could move. Something told me he easily could have taken my life, and again, it almost worried my more that he hadn't.

"Watch your back," I warned him one last time.

Then, before he could stop me, I ran towards the window, jumping through the glass and shattering it as I soared over the balcony to the grass two floors below. I hit the ground and rolled to break my fall before jumping back to my feet and pulling my cloaking spell around me again as I ran at the wall.

Guards were running toward the area I would have landed, though none were following me. Eyes burned into the back of my hooded head, and I knew that if I turned back, the Prince's eyes would be following me despite the spell. My lips pressed into a thin line as he confirmed what I had thought before.

A sharp pain in my leg let me know that I hadn't left through the window unscathed, but I wasn't going to worry about it now. I had done what I could for the Prince, it was up to him whether he would choose to believe me or not.

Though, I hoped he would choose to listen. It would be a shame for someone so kind and attractive to die for a sack of gold.

As soon as I made it to the trees, my conscience pinged at me. It was ridiculous how much it had been bugging me lately when I hadn't had this many issues since I was young. The alarms were still ringing out from the castle, yet my mind went to the shopkeeper from last night. The one the Prince had started to help by rebuilding his shop.

It was a stupid thought, one better left alone. But now that someone had managed to sneak into the palace, the Prince wasn't going to be able to leave and help him. Then my thoughts spiraled further, as I knew that not having his business to create income would be much more detrimental to him than those in the richer areas of the kingdom. It was a reminder of the way I had grown up in the guild, and I felt a pinch in my chest for stopping him from getting the help he needed.

I knew what it was like not to be able to support yourself, having to grow up relying on someone that would rather see you dead than help you. It wasn't pleasant, and the world wasn't kind to those that weren't able to help themselves.

Growling, I turned towards the village they had ventured to

last night. I wasn't going to be the cause of someone living on the streets, not when I could do something about it. That useless lump of muscle in my chest twisted as I thought about it. I would help the shopkeeper now, like I had hoped someone would have helped me. I would do something for him that I wasn't able to do for myself back then. And if that thought made my chest tighten with an unfamiliar emotion, then I ignored it.

The Guild Master was already going to kill me for my failure. The fact that an alarm had been sounded in the castle, and the Prince was still alive was enough reason to end my life, so what was a few hours longer while my death crawled ever closer?

I made my way towards the place I had followed the Prince and his friends just the night before. Reaching down and ignoring the pain it caused, I yanked the sharp glass piece from my leg and tossed it to the forest floor as I went. Then I pulled a line of bandage from my pack to tie around the wound that was now bleeding more profusely.

The bandage quickly turned red with blood, so I tied on another one, this time tighter, before continuing on towards my new destination.

If I was going to die by the Guild Master's hand tonight anyway, I would at least go out knowing that instead of ending a life, I had taken the time to make one better.

And that small piece of stupid muscle in my chest seemed to warm at the thought.

"The Prince wasn't able to make it, so he sent me in his

stead," I told the old man who was looking at me suspiciously.

While the Prince had worn a cloaking spell to get here, it seemed to be an open secret who was actually doing the work, and the people all over the kingdom seemed to love him.

I had been trying to convince the shopkeeper that I was here to help for the last twenty minutes. There was a part of me that didn't want to deal with the trouble this had already caused, but every time I tried to leave, my chest would twinge, and my memories would invade my head.

"Why would he send a girl to do a man's work?" the old man grumbled at me.

My shoulder's tensed, but I didn't let his words get to me. There were a lot of men that assumed I wasn't capable of hard work because I was a woman. I'd learned to move past it for the most part, though sometimes, like tonight, it seemed to get to me more.

I had heard it over and over in the guild, that a woman wasn't capable of killing as well as a man, but I thought that we were *more* capable. We were better able to keep a steady head when in a bad situation, and when it called for it, we could use the fact that men didn't think a woman capable to our advantage. We were also better at going unnoticed when needed.

The fact that there weren't as many women in the guild was because the men couldn't handle a woman doing the job, not that we couldn't do it.

"Do you want my help or not?" I asked him bluntly, not willing to stand around in the open and be berated when I was more than capable of going back to the guild to get the same treatment.

He seemed to think on it for longer than he should have, and I grunted before turning around, fully intending to leave him without help. It was a stupid idea anyway, I scoffed. What kind of assassin helps rebuild a shop?

"Fine," he gave in with a sigh, and I thought about telling him to screw off, that he had taken too long. "But I won't be responsible if you hurt yourself."

His gaze dropped to my thigh when I turned back around, and I could have sworn there was a level of concern in his gaze. It took me off guard, and at first I wasn't able to respond.

"Just show me where the supplies are and stay out of the way," whether he knew it or not, that small glimmer of concern had just ensured that I would finish this project before the sun rose.

It was the first time in as long as I could remember that someone seemed to care about my well-being, and as gruff as he seemed to be, the fact that he could care about a stranger made him a good person in my book. But this was going to be a long and hard process, and I was going to use everything that I had to make sure that he was able to open up his business the very next day.

"I can help rebuild my own shop," he said, disgruntled.

"You need to get your products together and make sure that you are ready to open tomorrow morning," I told him, walking towards the half-burned and roughly-patched structure.

"There's no way that we can finish this in one night," he denied, though I also saw a glimmer of hope in his eyes that said he wanted what I said to be true.

"Just sit back and watch this *woman* work." I told him, my voice not as hard as it normally was.

Before he could deny my words again, I stepped closer and examined the building from top to bottom, figuring out the steps that would need to be taken, and then figuring out the supplies I would need. Once I had created a plan and I knew what needed to be done, I would gather what I would need to do it. Creating the mental check list, I walked around grabbing what I needed until all the supplies were gathered, then I used my advanced speed and strength to get started.

I was an assassin, but that didn't mean that I was uneducated or unskilled. Even the things I wasn't taught I had made sure to teach myself. It was one of the reasons I was as good at killing as I was. I took every opportunity to learn what I could about anything and everything. From reading books, to watching others, I wasn't going to lose the chance to make myself better if I could help it.

So, with that thought and my plan in mind, I did what I told him I would, and fixed the building as good as new before the sun peaked in the sky the next morning.

He sat staring as I wiped the sweat from my brow, hands shaking with the exertion and pain it had taken to accomplish my goal. I had put everything I had into it, knowing that there was no use saving my strength when I didn't plan to survive through the day.

The thought that I should just not go back to the guild had passed through my head more than once, but what else was I supposed to do? Where was I supposed to go?

The guild was all I knew, and while I had a few other skills, I wasn't anything more than a killer at heart. There was no place in this world for a soul as dark as mine. While I was well known, it wasn't my face or name that people knew, only my reputation. If I tried to start over, I could probably get away with it, at least for a while. The guild wouldn't like its secrets being spilled, and they would never take my word that I wouldn't say anything.

Back stabbing and lies was just how they worked.

They would hunt me to the ends of the earth, and my death would be much more painful if that happened than if I returned now with just a failed mission under my belt.

The Guild Master was brutal, and I hated that he had power over me. I hated that he scared me.

But I would need to face him sooner or later, there was nothing else to do about it.

CHAPTER TWO

"THANK YOU SO MUCH, YOUNG LADY. I really didn't think you would be able to do it," the old man's words were full of gratitude, something that I wasn't used to hearing, even if it *was* a back handed compliment.

I shrugged, swallowing the uncomfortable feeling him thanking me created, and I pulled my hood further down over my face. He shouldn't have been able to see what I looked like, but I was feeling strangely vulnerable, and didn't quite know what to do.

"Your Prince wouldn't send someone he didn't think could do the job, would he?" I asked him like it was common sense.

It was only a guess on my part, but based on his actions over the last few weeks, and the assumptions that I had made based on what I had seen last night, I wouldn't think he would do anything less.

"You're right," the old man agreed with utter confidence. "I never should have doubted him."

I nodded, though I didn't really agree one way or another. It was time for me to go. I needed to leave before what I had done here was discovered and I was taken into custody. Either by the Prince, who would no doubt want to question me before he killed me, or by the guild members who would drag me back to certain death. But the other assassins would only do that after destroying this man's building and taking his life.

I wasn't going to sit around and wait for either of those things to happen, not now that my conscience was clear. At least, when it came to this man.

"You'd better hurry and open your shop," I said instead of a goodbye, turning to head into the forest.

Unfortunately, my leg chose that moment to rebel, and it went out from under me. Curses left my mouth as I stumbled and almost went down.

"Are you okay?" the old man asked, coming closer until a placed my hand up to stop him.

"I'm fine, just tired," I told him, my voice telling him not to argue. "I'll be on my way now."

He looked like he wanted to say something, but I ignored the expression and limped my way into the tree line. My leg was burning, and I couldn't use the working of my other muscles to ignore it any longer. My pants were soaked with blood, and the bandages were all soaked through as well. I had added two more as I worked, but the bleeding had only slowed enough that I knew I could still be in danger if I didn't stop it.

This may have been perfect though. If I could get far enough toward the guild before my body gave out, I may be able to play the injury card to get out of a death sentence. If they saw how badly I was bleeding, and then heard about the castle, maybe they would assume I was injured by the Prince and, though it was still a failed mission, it may just be enough to buy me my life.

It would also have the added benefit of giving the Prince more time to plan for an attack, assuming he had listened to me. There was still a lingering sense of doubt that he would listen, but he didn't seem stupid. He would be more on guard, even if he didn't take any other measures. The power I had sensed coming from him for that brief moment in time had made me think that may be enough to help him live no matter who they decide to send.

The sun was just about to start it's decent over the mountains when I knew I wouldn't be able to make it any farther. I hadn't made it far enough to be happy, but I also didn't think they would be looking for me so soon after a failure. It was well-known that if something was to go wrong, most people went to ground and hid until it was safe to continue on. Just because I hadn't done so yet, didn't mean that I wouldn't. But I had also never failed a mission before now, either.

Sliding down with my back pressed against a tree, I grimaced with pain as I stretched my legs out in front of me. Looking at my blood-soaked pant leg, and the now dripping red bandages should have alarmed me, but I was made of tougher stuff than this. While this may put me out for a day or two, it wasn't a life-threatening injury. Though, I needed to stop the bleeding and allow my advanced healing to kick in.

I drew a knife and cut the bandages away, then sliced my pant leg open so I could get a better look at the injury.

The glass had cut deep, but it hadn't hit anything important. I would have treated it sooner than this if it had.

I was familiar enough with my own body and the way that it handled injuries that I could almost always assess how bad it was at the time a blow was dealt. Time had taught me many things, and judging a wounds severity based on where it was and how it felt was one of them. It was a skill that I had developed over years of training, trial and error my only gage, and it wasn't something that I took lightly. I made sure to constantly listen to what my own body told me, knowing better than most that things could change in an instant.

I debated on what I wanted to do. I could stitch the wound and risk tearing it back open if I had to act swiftly, or I could cauterize the wound and have it hurt much worse if it reopened, yet, be more sturdy in the meantime.

The answer was an easy one; there was no way that I *wouldn't* be forced into some sort of action. Cauterizing it would also stop the bleeding which would help me to heal faster in the long run. I brought up the knife, summoning a flame in my other hand, and running the blade through it until it was glowing with heat. Then, when it was ready, I turned it and stabbed it into my own leg, both slicing it open more, and stopping the bleeding at the same time.

My breath escaped me in a hiss, but I didn't stop until the blade was cool and I was sure that I had managed to cover the whole injury.

"Well, that couldn't have been pleasant,"

I lurched to my feet, stumbling as I turned to face the threat I hadn't sensed coming.

My hand reached up unconsciously to make sure that my hood was still on, and I was relieved to find that it was. The spells that I used to hold it in place and hide my face were in full effect.

"You found me faster than I expected," I said, looking at the Prince and his friends as they stood in a triangle before me.

He only smiled, and I noted again how handsome he was, his friend's attractiveness complimenting him well. It was unusual to have so many high society men that were as attractive as them. Ones that weren't trying to undercut each other to make sure that they had a better choice of the women they bedded.

"It helped that you stopped to help old man Jack with his shop," the knight said, curiosity in his voice.

My gaze switched between the three men before me as well as my surroundings while I avoided saying anything else. My voice changing spell wasn't in place, and my words before hadn't been hidden. I had never let someone sneak up on me before, and it was making me jumpy. If they were able to get drop on me so easily, then the guild members may be able to as well. And that didn't bode well for either of us.

"And on order of the Prince himself," his advisor, a well-known magic user said with humor. "You must be good at your job if the Prince *himself* sent you."

I smiled despite myself at the teasing in his tone, even though they wouldn't be able to see it.

"Eh, I had nothing to lose, why not use the Prince's name?" I said with a shrug.

Something in the Prince's face darkened, and I almost wanted to take a step back. But I also instinctively knew that would be a bad idea. You never showed weakness to a predator, and I had a feeling that was exactly what this royal was. Though what kind, I wasn't sure.

I knew it wasn't smart, I also had to get out of here, bum leg or no. Not only was the Prince here, but if the guild members were on their way to get me, and they found him here as well, it would defeat the purpose of what I had done. And it would ruin my plans to try and stop my own death.

Giving the Idiot Brigade in front of me one last glance, I put their faces in my memory to think on later. Attractive men that were skilled enough to not only find me, but catch up to me were hard to find, and I wanted to remember this moment.

I turned, bunching my legs beneath me, and leapt up into the trees without saying another word. Leaping the long distance between branches and ignoring both the calls of surprised from below, as well as the pain running through my body. I really had used a lot of strength and speed to build that shop, and my body was letting me know that it wasn't happy about the way I was treating it.

Pulling on my senses and using them to sharpen my focus, I allowed a little bit more magic to flow through me. It increased the distance that I could jump, as well as the speed in which I moved. I still needed to look for sturdier branches to push off of, but less time on the branch meant that they didn't need to be big enough to support my full weight. I was already flying onto the next one by the time it had decided if it wanted to snap or not.

Just when I felt I was getting far enough away, my leg decided to give out again. I wasn't able to stick the landing and my body kept going. So, instead I tripped over the branch I had meant to land on and started to fall head first to the ground. I turned my body as best I could to minimize impact, but when I landed, I landed *hard*.

I release a whoosh as the air was knocked out of me, and my whole body throbbed with the pain of impact. My leg was useless at this point, and I wanted to growl in frustration. The cloaking spell I was using fell with my abrupt landing, and I sat up as the sound of feet in the underbrush reached me. The fact that the Prince and his men were silent let me know that it wasn't them.

"Look who we found, boys!" a familiar voice spoke as four men stepped into view. "Just who we were looking for."

The voice belonged to another guild member, and one of the main three that had plagued me since my reluctant enlistment.

Forcing myself to my feet, I ignored the pain and focused on the men that were circling me. They were like vultures seeking a fresh kill, and I kept my senses sharp so that I wouldn't be caught unaware. My eyes flashed to one of the men on the team, knowing that he was the reason they had been able to find me in the first place.

He was able to see glimpses of things that were going to happen, and as this was the first time my cloaking spell had been brought down unwillingly, it would have put out enough magical energy for him to pick up on. He would have been able to see me appear in this exact spot before it ever happened.

"What are you doing, Brock?" I asked the leader of the group, looking away from the other man. "Your father wouldn't be happy if he knew you were here. It hasn't even been a week yet."

I knew that he was about to try and kill me, but I wasn't sure if it was his choice, or the Guild Masters.

"Oh, I know," he said, and something about his smug tone told me that this situation was about to go from bad to worse. "We heard that you had failed. Which was curious, because you've *never* failed."

His voice was mocking as he paused, all four of them exchanging sneered smiles as they started to circle me like a pack of wolves who had scented their pray. I stayed still, not wanting to make a move before I had more information. It would be dumb to give this chance away. And aside from that, I had been bleeding for almost a whole day, something that would have killed a human by now. The problem was Brock's ability.

The rest of his team had lower level skills, as the man didn't like to be shown up, but he was the most dangerous to me right now.

"How does one lowly *Prince* escape the best assassin in the guild? My father's pride and joy? And why would that same Prince follow her into the forest?"

My eyes lit on his figure as he came back around in front of me. So, he knew, or at least he suspected, that it wasn't just a failed mission.

"Are you accusing me of something?" I asked him, wanting him to come right out and say it.

If he had followed me, that meant that either the Guild Master had been planning to kill me all along, or he was taking the opportunity to do it while he had an excuse. Even if he wasn't sure of what I had done, he had enough evidence to support any story he could come up with. Between that and the word of the men that were still surrounding me, my death at his hands would seem justified. Whether the Guild Master wanted it or not.

"I'm sure I'll think of something, but right now I don't care what happened," he said confirming at least that he wasn't sure that anything *had* happened. "But you won't have to worry, because you'll already be dead."

With the last word he lunged at me, the other three moving to attack at the same time.

Their weapons were drawn, and I twisted, bringing my cloak up to help hide the way my body was moving as I drew some knives of my own. My leg didn't want to work right, so that took the option to run off the table. This was going to have to be fast, and I couldn't let them get an opening or I was done for.

Two of the four men went down easily enough, my hand covered in warm, sticky blood from where I had sliced one man's throat and stabbed the other in the stomach. A slit throat was almost impossible to come back from, no matter what you were, but Brock and the fourth man were better trained, and from the way they fought together it was clear that they had teamed up before.

I jumped back out of their reach so I could have both men in front of me, careful not to rest too much weight on my injured leg. The way that their eyes flashed to the wound made it clear that it was something both men had made note of.

This should have been easy, taking them out should have been child's play. But they were just standing there, and my body was moving more sluggishly than before. A sharp slice of pain I hadn't noticed during the fight, and the wound on my leg had started bleeding again. It was flowing faster and in larger quantities than when I had gotten it, my head going light as my stomach heaved. The dizzying sensation was familiar. Blood loss.

I realized what was happening, and I remembered why I was always so weary around Brock. Just like his father, he was a master at manipulating things, and he specialized in blood. He could manipulate it once his target was bleeding. And even a small gash would have been enough, but my wound was much more than that. It was fresh enough that he forced it open with a sharp pain, and large amounts of blood started to run down my leg.

My head was starting to get hazy and my body was getting heavier by the moment. I needed to finish him fast, or I was going to pass out, and soon after he would finish me off.

"It was so nice of you to give me this opening," he taunted me, stepping closer as he loomed over me, even though I was still on my feet. "It's about time someone was able to take you down a peg."

"We both know you couldn't take me in a fair fight. Don't pretend that you weren't waiting for something like this to happen." I snarled at him, trying to force the hazy feelings away long enough to attack.

His face twisted when I spoke, knowing it was the truth even if he wanted to deny it. There was a reason his own father gave *me* the higher paying jobs.

"Now, you die!" he screamed at me, him and his teammate

lunging at me once more.

I wouldn't be able to dodge both of them, not with my leg in such a state. So instead I just dodged the worst of it, allowing Brocks blade to enter my side the barest amount. He smiled in victory, but he was in my range now. His teammate missing me completely as I stepped closer to my target.

"Goodbye, Brock," I said softly.

Then with one swift move I slid my dagger along his throat, flipping the knife, and turning the slightest bit to slam my blade back into his friend's stomach as he tried to back away. I dragged the knife down and out as he stumbled back, watching as his innards fell to the ground before me while Brock's body fell lifelessly at the same time.

The second man fell right after, and I winced as I pulled Brock's blade from my side. That cloudy feeling had taken over my head again, and though the wound on my leg was back to bleeding at a normal pace, I was now dealing with two cuts and a worn-out body. Just what I needed right now.

My head tilted, as something, not a sound, but *something*, alerted me to the fact that I now had three more visitors.

My shoulders fell a bit as I knew I wasn't going to be able to take them on as well, especially with how I was feeling right now. That left trying to run, and I wasn't sure how far I would make it before they caught up to me. Blood loss was dangerous, even for me. It wouldn't kill me on its own, but it left me vulnerable while I passed out. So, it was like putting a sign over my head that said 'please kill me'.

"Do you always cause so much trouble?" the advisor asked, the humor still in his voice, though it was almost buried under concern.

A sigh escaped me, and I decided that I needed to try and run, even if only to make myself feel better about the death that was sure to find me.

"Yeah," I answered, my voice much more tired that I had ever heard it.

Leaping into the trees was out; I wouldn't be able to take another tumble. That meant I needed to distract them with something while I ran away. Not able to think of anything better to do, I turned towards the three men that were standing a short distance behind me, realizing as I did that my hood had fallen back during the fight sometime, and it was no longer covering my face.

I drew a line of fire between us, forcing it to rise high enough that it all I could see of them were shadows, and I hoped that they hadn't gotten a good enough look at my face that they would remember it as I turned to run.

Pulling my cloak up around me once more, I took to the forest, leaving the bodies of my late comrades to be taken care of by the forest itself. I forced my leg to carry me, knowing that at this point I was bound to be causing more harm than good. That didn't stop me, though, and I ran as fast as my failing body could take me.

There was only one place to go, even if I could never think of it   as   my   home.

CHAPTER THREE

THEY WERE TRACKING ME, AND I NEEDED to figure out how they were doing it, and fast. I turned in the direction I knew a stream flowed and kept going. My body was rebelling with every step, and I wanted nothing more than to stop and collapse into a pile on the ground, but that wasn't an option.

The sound of water grew closer, and instead of a slow trickling stream, I found a river waiting for me. It didn't look to be going very fast, but looks were deceiving, and I didn't know how deeply it ran. My magic was the only thing holding me up at this point, and I didn't want to use it for anything else in case I had to use it to fight later on.

There wasn't time to think about that though, as I ran straight into the current. The freezing water stole my breath, and the pressure against my wounds when I kept going was horrifyingly painful.

Pressing on, I went as fast as I could down the center of the river, fighting my own body as well as the current. My eyes were fluttering as they tried to close, but I knew that I needed to walk farther before exiting on the other side. The water bringing comfort as well as pain as it tried to drag me down with it.

If one of them was able to track me by scent, then I needed to make it harder, if not impossible for them to smell me. If it was through magic, then I was already lost. The magic in my cloak should have hidden me from any spells that sought me out with ill intent. *And* most of the ones that looked for me with *good* intentions.

It didn't matter how they were doing it, only that I did everything I could to evade them. I just needed to hide long enough that I could have some time to heal. There wasn't a guarantee I would be able to take them on when I was healed, but I would have a better chance than I did right now.

Though, it was odd that they hadn't killed me yet. They'd had plenty of opportunities to do so. Then another thought took hold, and my chest went cold. Maybe they were planning to capture and torture me to see what I knew about the guild. It had been done before, and would be again. But, for some reason, the thought of any of those men using pain to try and force answers from me made me sick to my stomach. And it wasn't the thought of pain, that did it, but the *men*.

Did I think that one warning would be enough to ensure some good will? I liked to think that I wasn't that naive. I had watched them all for weeks, plotted out way after way to kill the Prince, and some part of me thought that because I had warned him instead of killing him that I wouldn't deserve to be tortured for information?

That was a stupid thought, and I wasn't going to allow it anymore energy.

From now on, I would assume only that they were after me to kill me or gather information. Nothing else.

If only I could believe it will my whole heart, and not just most of it.

I collapsed in a wet, pain-filled puddle in the hollow of a tree, shivering and bleeding. I had gone as far as I could. Not even my will was enough to carry me any farther. I hoped it had been enough, but common sense and experience told me that it wasn't.

It all came down to which would happen first. Would they find me before I could heal? Or would I be able to rest and heal enough to keep going?

"If you keep running like this, I'm going to start thinking you don't like me," the Prince said, bending down to peer at where I was huddled in the tree.

I snorted a laugh, too tired to stop it.

"Running away in horror is usually a good indication that a girl doesn't like you," I agreed.

He smiled back at me and I wasn't sure where they words had come from. It wasn't like me to make jokes; I was more the type to sit quietly and observe those around me. There was never any time for me to find a sense of humor.

A snort of laughter came from behind him and I cursed myself for not staying on my guard. I needed to do something. Try to continue running, fighting, *something*.

The Prince backed up as I slowly and painfully made my way out from under the tree. My whole body shook with the effort, the wind cutting through my wet clothes and the cold trying to steal the rest of my energy as well as my warmth. My breaths were little more than pants, and I had my arm pressed against the cut in my side that had yet to stop bleeding. My legs shook with the effort it took to stand, but I painstakingly made it to my feet.

Drawing a knife, I held it shakily in front of me while all three men watched with amused exasperation.

"So, you *do* still have some fight left in you," the knight said with a smile. "That's good."

I wasn't sure what to make of his words, but he didn't draw the sword at his side, and he left his other weapons alone as well.

"Yes, it's all well and good that she's a fighter, now can we leave before she hurts herself even worse?" the Prince's advisor grumbled. "We should get back before the sun sets, or the whole castle is going to try and mount a rescue mission."

"By all means," the Prince said, stepping away and gesturing towards me.

I brought the blade up, assuming that meant the advisor would be my first opponent, but instead of drawing a weapon, he rolled his eyes with a smile and stepped towards me. I swung, but missed when I moved too slowly and he was able to dodge my attack with ease. Placing his palm on my forehead over my hood before I was able to counter, he looked me straight in the eyes. Shock traveled through me, and my eyes widened.

He shouldn't be able to see me under my cloak.

My knife hesitated as I met his gaze, something warm and unfamiliar making me pause at his touch. The feeling made me shake worse than before, and I lost my focus as I looked back at the mage.

"Sleep," he whispered softly, and it was too late for me to counter his spells effects.

I cursed and tried to jerk away, but my eyes were already closing, my body falling uselessly to the ground.

Strong arms caught me before I could meet the earth, and I

was lifted against a chest that felt too hot against my cold skin. The sensation of being in someone else's arms was an unfamiliar one, and the Prince smelled of woodsmoke and cinnamon, something that I would have thought to be unpleasant. But it was the opposite, and I had to work twice as hard to fight of the mage's spell.

"Well done, Merrick," the Prince's words rumbled against my head as it was pressed into his chest.

He started to walk and my whole body seemed to bounce with his steps. His heat seeped into my side, relieving some of the pain flowing through me even as I fought the spell trying to put me under. I wasn't going to win, I knew it, and they knew it, but I was going to try.

"Just because I'm not at your level yet, doesn't mean I'm useless in a fight," Merrick scoffed.

"That wasn't much of a fight," the knight said with humor.

The sound of flesh meeting flesh was followed shortly by a chuckle.

The familiar noise sent my pulse skyrocketing with remembered fear, and I slowly brought the knife they hadn't thought to take from me up, pressing it against the skin of the Prince's chest. I could feel him looking down at me, even though I wasn't able to open my eyes in more than a squint, but his steps didn't falter.

Even though I pressed the knife against his flesh, my hand shook and I couldn't bring myself to harm him. Someone with a soul as good as the one he had didn't deserve to be killed so someone like me could live.

My hand fell to my lap, knife unused.

Another chuckle came from above me, and a spot of warmth seemed to light upon my forehead.

"Just rest, Kitten, everything will be alright."

"You're wrong," I whispered, but if he said anything else, I didn't hear it.

My eyes closed and I wasn't able to fight off the spell's effects any longer.

I woke the next morning surprised that I was waking up at all. But I was even more shocked to find that I wasn't bound in any way.

What kind of people take a prisoner and don't take them to the dungeons immediately? And if they weren't going to do that, why wouldn't they bind me and take my things away? I was still wearing my cloak, and all of my weapons were in their correct places.

My eyes roamed around the room I was in, and I took note of the chest of drawers across from the bed I had woken in. A large desk sat in the corner of the room; a comfortable looking chair placed before it.

It was odd, not being bound and under guard, but I was going to take advantage of the opportunity they had given me.

I stood and didn't bother to check the door, knowing that they probably had someone posted to watch the room, even if they were at the end of the hall. No, it would be faster and easier to leave out the window.

Standing, I winced as pain radiated from both my injuries. Testing my weight and movements let me know that they were going to cause problems, but I would have to deal with that once I had escaped.

The window latch was already unlocked, and something about that made me hesitate. This was too easy. Something else had to be going on here. So, what was I missing? Why hadn't they locked me up? Why had they made it so easy to escape after they had gone through the trouble of tracking me down not once, but *twice*?

Fully expecting a trap, I tensed as I opened the window and stepped back, ready for something to happen.

Only...nothing did.

There wasn't a single spell or alarm that went off.

It should have been reassuring, but all I felt was more unsettled.

Nothing in my life was easy, and there was no way that someone like me would be getting off without a scratch, not after what I had done.

Choosing to ignore my misgivings for now, I looked over the ledge of the window seal and to the grass two levels below. My leg hurt just looking at the jump, but I didn't see anybody in view. As I looked at the people outside, I noticed that the guards were doing their normal rotations. Nothing seemed to have changed since the last time I had been here, and despite myself, I frowned.

Movement caught my eye, and I looked over just in time to see one of the guards stationed at the end of the building look away from me.

So, they were aware that I was here, and they were looking out for my escape attempt. But that still didn't explain why they were making this so easy.

I ducked back inside the room, pulling my hood more securely around my face and casting a spell to cloak my movements. I would be leaving without being seen, or I would die trying. I was too tired to keep the spell up for long, and I would need to run fast on my bad leg without having it give out.

Both things, annoying alone, were infuriating together.

I *hated* being weak.

This was going to be much more difficult than it should have been thanks to my injuries. This whole situation was making me tense as I was waited for the other shoe to drop. My leg was on fire, but everything else until now had been going *too* well.

Grumbling under my breath, I looked at the window once more, and as soon as I visualized what I wanted to do, I ran and jumped.

My body soared over the ground, taking me a good distance from the building before I hit the ground and rolled. I had to bite my lip to keep a pained sound from escaping, shakily forcing myself to my feet and holding my side. Pain wouldn't stop me, not today, not ever.

The guard watching my room didn't seem concerned, and he hadn't noticed my escape yet either. It was odd, but he seemed to be human, so I wasn't going to blame him for not seeing me when the spell flickered upon landing. He wasn't looking this way, after all.

I made it to the wall without issue, still feeling like this was going too smoothly. Even if my leg was already begging me to stop.

Instead of jumping to the top of the wall, I climbed it, mostly using my arms to take some of the pressure off my legs. Both wounds would heal soon enough. The only reason they were causing me such problems right now was because Brock had messed with them. His magic was like a virus my body hadn't yet rid itself of. His magic had faded with his life, but the effects would linger a while longer yet.

It was the blood loss that was the biggest issue. I had already lost quite a bit before I had come across him, and he had just made it worse. Annoyance once again flickered at the thought that he had been able to get so close to beating me. It was something that wouldn't have normally been an issue, and I berated myself for allowing it to happen. I shouldn't have pushed myself so hard working on that man's shop. Then I would have healed just fine and I would have easily beat the blood manipulator.

Finally arriving at the top of the wall, I was worried my absence would be noticed sooner rather than later. I looked back once to see that I still hadn't been found missing, and even knowing what a bad idea it was, I jumped down on the other side. The impact made my teeth clench in pain, but I stayed on my feet, so I was counting it as a win.

"I told you she would try and escape," a smug male voice said from a short distance down the wall.

I turned to look at the three men that were leaning there, waiting for me. Not wanting to give them a chance to grab me again, I started to run.

I didn't make it much more than ten steps before someone grabbed me around the waist. I drew a knife on instinct but stopped myself before I could drive it into my captor's side. Why couldn't I bring myself to harm them? What was it about them that made causing them injury seem worse than being tortured to death at their hands?

Cursing, I put the blade back and instead summoned a bit of fire to my hands. The knight swore and dropped me at the heat I held to his arms. As soon as my feet hit the ground, I pushed on, only to run into a wall. Well, not a wall, just the Prince's chest. But it sure felt like a solid surface.

The man was too silent for his own good. I was usually the one catching others off guard. Having that skill used against me wasn't fun, though I had to admit that something inside me was thrilled at the unexpected notion that someone *could* do it. There was always some part of me that hated being the best in the guild, hated not having someone I considered an equal when it came to my skills. I never would have imagined finding someone that was *better* than me.

My body dropped before he could grab me, and I rolled backwards and back to my feet, lunging forward and out of the knight's reach. The advisor was just watching with an amused face as I made it around both the knight and the Prince.

A wall of fire appeared before me, much like the one I had used last night. I smiled back at the advisor as he held his hand out, the magic in the wall his. It was a nice try, but fire was *mine* to control.

With a smirk that he couldn't see from under my cloak, I stepped right into the flames, letting them surround me with their powerful energy and warmth. All my pain disappeared, only to reappear once I stepped out on the other side.

The wall disappeared almost as soon as it appeared, disbelief and something else on the advisor's face as he looked to the Prince. I didn't bother to stick around to try and figure out what it was. Instead I ran as fast as my now partially healed wounds would let me. Merrick's magic having helped speed the healing a bit.

The trees went passed me in a blur, and as soon as I was able to find an opening in the branches above me, I jumped. Then I started running through the treetops, hoping from tree to tree. They would be hard pressed to keep up with me today. Even though I wasn't at full speed, I was much lighter and faster than any human ever would be.

I wasn't sure any of the three men that I had just run from were fully human, but I was born to be one with the trees. The forest was my domain, the elements my brothers and sisters. This was my home much more than any house ever could be.

It was only too bad that it wasn't safe to stay here with the

Guild Master and other assassins on the loose.

CHAPTER FOUR

AFTER MY FAILED MISSION WITH THE prince three months ago, the Guild Master hadn't allowed me more than a few hours to rest before giving me a new contract to fulfill. And my new mission was going to get me killed. But with everything else that had been happening, I was starting to think that was the point.

When I had made it back to the guild after my botched job, it was to find an incredibly surprised Guild Master. Then, before I could even breathe, he handed me another job that wouldn't give me any time to heal. Thankfully, it was an easier job than anticipated, and I didn't have any trouble taking out the lowlife that was praying on the night workers of a distant city.

But this job, this might just be the one to kill me.

I was fully healed, and I had been training harder than ever, even if I had to do it outside the guild hall. The Guild Master wouldn't like knowing how much I was able to improve after just being around the Prince and his friends for a few moments. And with the way he was acting, I wasn't inclined to tell him.

The Idiot Brigade didn't really do much, they just showed me how complacent I had gotten with the way things were. How much I had let being the best in the guild fool me into thinking that meant I was actually the *best*. It was stupid and vain, and I wasn't going to let myself fall into that same prideful place from before.

"Well, are you going to kill me or not, scum?" the man before me hissed.

He was stealing money from the people of his lands, and though it wasn't much, they were suffering without it. They had spent the rest of what they had in order to place the price on his head, and this job was one that I was going to enjoy carrying out.

After watching him and learning his habits, I had found it wasn't just money he was stealing. He was working with the bandits outside his walls to make sure that his people weren't able to truly flourish. He was making sure they stayed reliant on him and his leadership.

That was about to end. Tonight, I would take his life, or I would die trying.

"Put the boy down and face me like a man," I growled at him, not willing to endanger the poor scared child any more than was necessary.

It was pathetic that he had grabbed a hostage in the first place. That he had picked a child to use against me spoke volumes about the kind of person he was. The problem, and what made me think that this mission was a ruse to get me killed, was the fact that he had known I was coming. And he had come prepared.

"What would be the fun of that?" he asked, but I could see the fear in his eyes.

The rumors of my skill had found their way here and, for

once, I was okay with that.

The men he brought with him shifted uncomfortably as they looked between me and their leader. They were shifters, and the pack was a decent size, but they didn't seem like they wanted to fight. Their alpha was weak enough on his own that he had felt the need to take a hostage. It looked bad for the man, and a few of his own pack didn't look too pleased with him at the moment.

That was good news for me. And them.

"Your pack's getting restless, you should probably step up soon, or it won't just be me you're fighting." My words were a taunt.

It was a white lie, but now the seed of doubt had been planted and I could tell that at least some part of him believed me. There must have been other issues before this, and my words were doing more damage than I had intended. A smile took over my face as I watched his eyes flick to the wolves around us. He wasn't just looking at me as the only threat now, his pack mates were on his list of people to watch out for.

I needed to be more careful now, however. He was an instinct fueled being, and shifters could be known to make rash decisions based more on feeling than logic. If he reacted too brashly and attacked them first, then I was going to have to act fast in order to get the boy to safety. If he attacked *me*, then I would have to hope I could do the same thing, but I would also have to worry about dodging his attacks all the while.

"They would never betray me," he denied, his voice not as sure as he wanted me to believe. "Now, fight me or leave!"

My eyes flicked around the clearing, trying to look for any way out that would leave both me and the boy alive at the end of this fight. So far, I wasn't feeling hopeful.

"What kind of coward hides behind a child?" I tried once more, using my cloak to cover my actions as I drew a knife.

43

"Even with all your men here to back you up, your still scared a girl is going to get the best of you? You have to use a child to make yourself feel like more of a man?"

His face went red with anger, his canines growing longer as a growl released from his chest. I had hit him straight in the pride, and that made him angry. He was an alpha, he was supposed to be the strongest one here, yet I had just called him weak in front of his entire pack.

The child in his arms whimpered in fear, the first sound he had made since he had been grabbed. It had surprised me that he had been so brave, but it looked like he was finally cracking under the pressure of his terror.

If he made himself look like prey to these wolves though...

I needed to get him out of here.

The little boy's eyes were wide, and I could all but smell his fear. It would be stronger to the wolves' noses.

Movement from behind alerted me to the fact that someone was coming, the brief flicker of the alpha's eyes a warning of which direction the attack was going to come from.

Cursing, I ducked and drew a knife, thrusting it up and into the stomach of the wolf that was attacking me. The move unbalanced me enough that I rolled onto my back, using the momentum and my knife to throw his now lifeless body into the wolves at my back.

The alpha was forced to release the boy to get out of the way, and a quick bit of magic was the only thing that stopped the boy from being crushed. He screamed as he was flung up to the sky, but after the initial surge, my magic gently carried him up and into the topmost branches of the nearest tree.

Saving him cost me time, and before I could fully get out of the way the alpha was coming at me.

We rolled, and I swung my blades at him, barely missing when he leapt back away from me. I rolled back and onto my feet, getting into a stance that would better let me defend myself. The boy was out of the way, I wouldn't have any trouble getting rid of the alpha now. I just hoped that the rest of the pack would leave me alone afterwards. It wasn't likely, but the hope was still there.

My eyes roved over the gathered men, noting their positions and the best ways out for when I finished this fight. Most of the men still didn't look happy at what was happening, but this was their alpha. Unless I took care of him out quickly, they were obligated to protect him to the death. Theirs, or his.

With my distraction out of the way and safe, there was no reason for me to linger and fight him. Pulling another knife, this one rougher-looking and smaller, I turned and threw it at the charging alpha, aiming for his heart.

He wasn't able to dodge a blade that was so fast, and it punctured his chest, sinking in only a few inches before stopping. It wasn't deep enough to penetrate his heart. And I knew I wouldn't be getting another shot.

He howled in pain, his face contorting with his rage and I knew that I would need to think fast in order to survive his next attack. His pack was gearing up to take me on, and I needed to act before they could.

Instead of removing the blade, the alpha just started to run at me again. I dodged to the side and then had to jump to avoid the wolf behind me. Some of the others started to shift, their clothing shredding in odd places as they did so, and one part of me was fascinated at the same time it was disgusted.

Magic filled the air as they started to change, and the feel of pressure was oppressive as their bodies were torn apart and then put back together in a different way. The process was fascinating...if I didn't have to watch it happen in front of me.

The alpha started to growl as his body got taller, fur grew from his pours as his arms and legs shifted to more closely resemble those of a wolf, his knees now bending backward. But after that, his shift stopped, and he stayed standing on two feet.

And just like that, I realized why the pack would allow someone so cruel and twisted to lead them. He was a one of those powerful enough to half shift. The word powerful wasn't necessarily the right word to use, more like he was lucky. It was a trick of the genes that allowed some to partially shift while others could only access one form. It was different depending on the species of shifter, but wolves were the most common, and yet the least likely to be able to do a half shift.

It also explained why my dagger hadn't gone any deeper into his chest. His muscles would be more built up from the constant half shifting, his body automatically protecting his most vulnerable bits. What would have killed a normal human, or even shifter, did nothing but annoy the man charging at me.

My feet hit the ground, but I hardly had time to land before I was hit behind the knees. I flipped over backwards, training and instinct kicked in allowing me to hit the ground with my hands and flip to land on my feet. Though I had to jump again immediately to dodge another attack from the other side.

The blows were coming fast, and I was left dodging him as I thought about my next move. I needed to get into a better position to defend myself if I was going to have to take them all on at once. My mind focused and my senses sharpened as I took in my opponents, taking this situation seriously for the first time since I arrived to find a veritable army facing me.

More wolves came at me, putting me on the defensive, and I poured half my focus into the fight, the other half spent checking on the boy who hadn't moved or made a sound since my magic had taken him up to the trees. I wouldn't put it past the alpha to try and use him against me again. Even now when I could all but feel how smug he was at the situation.

He was so sure that they were going to win, that they would be able to overpower me soon enough. Cool, calmness flowed through me, even when one of the wolves got in a lucky hit and a cut was opened up on my arm.

The world suddenly seemed to freeze as the feeling that something was coming swept over me.

Magic, powerful and overwhelming surged up around us, and my fight or flight instincts flared up at the threatening feeling that was settling in the air. A few of the wolves seemed to sense it too, as they stopped fighting to start looking around the small clearing that we found ourselves in.

The moon was high overhead, but it suddenly seemed dull in comparison to the impending doom that was coming for us.

Locating the alpha, I found that he was looking around like most of his wolves, forgetting the threat that was right in front of him. Taking the opportunity, I pulled a long, beautifully carved branch, watching as it grew the slightest bit, a line of string connecting the two ends to create a bow. An arrow appeared as I drew it back and ran at the alpha. Aiming just past his head, I let the arrow fly. An arrow to the head isn't guaranteed to go deep enough to kill, especially a shifter with a half form, and I wasn't going to waste the effort.

It soared right past him, making him turn towards me with a growl. I smiled an unkind smile that he couldn't see, and taking the chance, I used one of his pack mates as a spring board to jump towards him. My foot landed on the blade in his chest, forcing it in farther as it grew a few inches to protrude out his back.

Time seemed to pause for a moment as we met gazes, his surprised, mine uncaring, as his eyes started to grow blank with death.

I used the leverage of his body to push off and jump up toward the boy in the trees. He let out a sound of surprise as I scooped him up and kept going. That feeling was coming closer, and I wanted to get out of here as soon as possible. I continued to jump through the trees, having to account for the boy's weight as well as my own when I leapt. His arms and legs curled around the front of my body as he clung to me.

The rest of the pack didn't worry me right now, so I just kept going until the feeling of threat faded. I didn't know what had caused the feeling, but I knew it wasn't something I wanted to deal with when I had to protect the small child in my arms. Or possibly at all.

I was moving in the opposite direction of the boy's house for a bit longer. The threat had been coming from the area I knew he lived, and I didn't want to chance it. Now, though, that feeling had faded, the forest returning to normal and the moon almost seeming to shine brighter. I figured whatever had caused the threat had gone.

Still, I didn't take a direct path back. The child in my arms cuddled in closer, no longer gripping me with fear, but more for comfort.

It was an odd sensation, to be cuddled by a child. Soon his eyes closed, and he dozed off, too worn out to stay awake. He had been through a lot tonight, and I couldn't blame him for sleeping. His slight weight in my arms sending an odd warmth to further burrow into my chest. The muscle there was getting a workout these days.

It wasn't too long before the sun set the next day that I arrived at the house I thought the boy had come from. I wasn't sure as I hadn't seen where the alpha had grabbed him, just that he had, and it had happened around here. But I waited in the trees to make sure that everything was okay. I didn't want to risk someone from the pack coming and taking him again. So, I settled on the branch, allowing the child to cuddle into me farther as I sat and waited for darkness to fall once more.

The moon was out, and a light was burning through the window as I gently fell from the tree's branches to land on the ground. My steps to the door were silent, and I took a deep breath before knocking.

Most people didn't respond well to a cloaked figure holding their child, especially after that child had been kidnapped, so I was ready for anything.

The door swung open to show a tired and worried man, the tear stained face of a woman peering out from behind his shoulder.

"My baby!" She screamed, pushing past the now surprised male.

Her loud exclamation woke the child in my arms, and he gripped me tighter as he was harshly woken up. The man grabbed the woman's arm to stop her from coming any closer to me, his face wary. My eyes dropped down to the boy in my arms as the man squared his shoulders like he was expecting a fight.

The boy was looking up at me, and I couldn't help the small smile that escaped me as his chubby cheeked face gazed at me so trustingly. He smiled back at me and started to calm down when he realized that we weren't under attack. He could see under my hood, and that should have worried me, but right now I didn't care.

I knelt on the ground, setting him on his feet, and turning him to face his family before his father could say anything. The child grabbed my arm tighter before he recognized the people we were standing in front of. Then, with a cry of surprised he ran towards his parents, tears trailing down his face for the first time since everything had happened. He was finally safe.

"Who are you?" the man asked me with nervous surprise as he bent to wrap his arms around his child and his weeping wife.

"Your son is very brave," I told him instead of answering. "You should be proud."

He opened his mouth like he was going to respond, but I had lingered long enough. Jumping up over them and onto their roof, I used the rest of the buildings as steppingstones through the village until I got back to the edge of the forest. My body nothing more than a silhouette to anyone that may see me.

At least I had been able to get the job done and save the boy. The Guild Master was trying to kill me, that much was almost a given, but I still didn't have anywhere else to go. And the anger in my chest wanted me to walk up to the man I had been forced to serve for years and ask *why*?

As I ran through the forest, switching between the treetops and the ground, I debated on what to do. There wasn't any place for me to go, not that wouldn't also result in my death. If I went back to the guild, the Guild Master would just give me another assignment to take care of. But at the same time, what else did I have to do?

He was going to do his best to kill me whether I went back or not, at least this way I would be able to take out a few evil people along the way. What more could an assassin ask for?

Slowing down, I decided I would rest for the night. God knew he wouldn't allow me to rest before sending me back out on another job. I needed to get some sleep while I could.

Tomorrow, and the rest of my short life, was going to be rough.

CHAPTER FIVE

I WAS RIGHT. THE GUILD MASTER gave me another case as soon as I stepped through the door.

"This one needs to be done as soon as possible; you don't have time to rest." Jyria said, a vicious smile pulling on the scar that sat at the corner of his lips.

"Yes, sir," I said, that same pull in my mind that always accompanied one of his orders.

It was a threat as much as a promise, and I had to ignore the fear that sensation caused to build inside me so that my voice didn't shake. There was an equal mix of anger when I looked at the man, and I knew that if it was possible, I would have killed him years ago.

But that was nothing more than wishful thinking. He waved a hand at me, dismissing me without another word, and I turned on my heel to leave the large chamber he used to conduct business and assign jobs.

I would do what I always did. I would plot and plan his

death, doing my best to survive, and pretend that I had a chance of actually accomplishing either goal.

One day he would die, and it would be by my hand. That was a promise.

My next few assignments were more difficult, and I was getting frustrated with Guild Master Jyria, wondering why he wasn't just outright trying to kill me himself.

At the same time, I knew that he couldn't without the rest of the guild getting suspicious of his intentions. If he was willing to outright kill someone that had done everything ordered of her, then what would stop him from going after those that had messed up even a little? Nothing.

Not that he ever allowed mistakes to be made, but everyone worked differently, and sometimes there was collateral damage. At least, that's what they called it.

"This needs your immediate attention," Jyria said, and I nodded as I took the offered parchment. "I don't like how long your assignments have been taking. Do you need a refresher course on why you need to be better?"

His words were a soft growl, the tension in the back of my head a warning, and despite my best effort, fear filled me. He didn't have another reason to go after me, so he was starting to stoop to threats to see if it would make me mess up. And there was a part of me that worried it would work.

"No, sir," I said, trying to keep my words clam even if my heart was trying to beat its way out of my chest.

Then, not saying another word, I turned and left his chamber without waiting to be dismissed. A stupid move after receiving a threat, but I wanted to do something under my own power, and that was all I could get away with.

"Did you hear that the Guild Master is sending someone else

after the Prince?" One of the other assassins said as I passed him in the hall, his eyes flicking to me as he talked to another member.

I knew this man, and I didn't think he was a bad person. Though this behavior was odd. It was almost like he was trying to warn me. But why would he do that? And what connection did he think I had to the Prince?

I slowed my steps, enhancing my hearing so I could try and get more information.

"Yeah, since the freak screwed up, I heard he's sending in a team to get the job done." His associate said.

"Yeah, but if the Prince is so protected that even *she* failed, how do they expect to be able to kill him tonight?" The first man said as they got farther away.

"She's not perfect, she's just a disgrace that should have been..."

They got too far away for me to hear anything more, but I had heard enough. Someone was going after the Prince, and they were going to do it tonight.

I looked down at my own assignment, looking over the details but not really seeing anything as my heart started to pound. For some reason, the thought that the Prince was in danger was making me anxious.

Shaking my head, I started to walk away. He was perfectly capable of taking care of himself, that wasn't the issue, but I still felt like it was my job to protect him, which was stupid. My job was to *kill* people, not save them.

And yet, I couldn't seem to get over the urge when it came to the three men I had met at the castle.

Blowing out a hard breath, I finally looked down at the parchment in my hands. My eyes took in the details, and a smile came to my face as a plan started to form in my head. My next target was a man that I already knew was no good, no research required. But the best part was that he lived inside the city right below the Prince's castle.

If I could get this done fast, then I may be able to stop the assassination attempt on the Prince as well. It was still early enough in the morning that, if I used my magic to get there, then I could pull this off.

Stopping by my quarters, I grabbed all of my weapons, not leaving a single thing behind. My weapons and thin armor both glowed at my touch, settling on my body as I prepared myself for a fight. I didn't always wear my full armor, but if I was going to go against three of the guilds best, then I wasn't going to take any chances.

My eyes glanced at the three other sets of armor I had crafted, but I shook my head. I didn't need those right now.

Dressed and ready, I pulled my cloak back around me, the hem brushing the ground but enchanted not to get underfoot. The hood was also enchanted to cast a shadow over my face when it was pulled up, and it was a lot harder to make it fall off than a normal cloak would be. My favorite part of the whole thing, though, was that it didn't really block my vision, just made the area around me a bit darker. My night vision more than made up for the difference when I used it at night, and it didn't hinder my movements at all.

Not wasting time, I left the guild building as soon as I was ready, using my speed to run through the forest and to the city that sat just below the castle on the hill. It was a trip that took a day for a human to walk, but it took me only a few hours. I looked up at the large castle that was clearly visible up on its hill.

The building was large, and beautiful. The brick and stone on the outside a creamy white color and the rest of the features, a stark contrast with the colors dark purple, light lavender, and black. The flags were a light lavender with the image of a dragon in black and white on it. Its tail brought up to make it a circle, wings up and fire spewing from its mouth. The image made me smile, and I felt like those in the castle may have had more secrets than the guild expected.

As I entered the town proper, I pulled on my cloaking spell. This would ensure that others wouldn't be able to see me as I made my way toward the house holding my target.

I had found out about this man on one of my previous jobs, but going after him on my own would have been a death sentence if the Guild Master had ever found out. I had even thought about placing a price on his head myself, but that would have been traced back to me eventually as well. And with all my money held by the guild, it wasn't like I would be able to access the funds to pay regardless.

It wasn't that other assassins didn't kill people as collateral, but there was a higher standard set for me, especially now that the Guild Master was looking for a reason to take me out. One mistake, and he would use it as a reason to kill me. No one would fight him on it for my sake, not when almost all of them hated me just as much as he seemed to. Fear for themselves would be what upset them if he killed me without reason. It was why he had been so careful until now. He couldn't afford an uprising in the ranks. Even his power could only go so far.

Stepping up in front of the door to the house, I wondered how something so nice could be the home of a man like my target. The stonework was impeccable, and he had his own coat of arms that had been chiseled into a special colored stone above all the doorways. It was a sign of how wealthy he was, and most of that fortune had been made through less than reputable ways.

Walking around to the back, I easily leapt over the short wall that lead to his small garden. There was a crying woman kneeling over one of the beds as she pulled the food items that she could. A large, dark bruise was still appearing on her cheek, and a small cut was still weeping blood on her lip.

I narrowed my eyes at the sight, my resolve hardening further. I didn't enjoy taking lives, but I had also managed to reason away most of my guilt by proving to myself that my targets were bad people that deserved death. This time I wouldn't need to reason it out, the proof was sobbing before me.

Walking past the woman, I ignored the fact that the sun was still high in the sky. I didn't have the time to wait for it to get dark if I wanted to stop the men going after the Prince. It was going to be hard enough as it was without trying to play catch up with them, and I didn't want anyone from the castle to know I had been there.

I didn't bother to continue cloaking my presence as I entered the house. A woman that was in the kitchen released a startled yelp at the sight of my cloaked figure walking in. She covered her mouth as soon as the sound escaped, and a look of regretful fear appeared as she looked at the doorway. Her eyes were wide as she seemed to forget that I was even there.

The action was telling, letting me know she was more worried about the master of the house's punishment than the threat of a cloaked figure entering the house. She feared the man over the possibility of death.

The sound of pounding steps came toward us, anger present in every step.

The young woman was trembling, tears starting to gather in her eyes as they were held hostage by the empty passage. I was completely forgotten as she was held hostage by her terror.

I stopped just inside the kitchen as the steps got closer, leaning at the side of the doorway with my blade at the ready. I was out of view of the man that was stomping his way towards us, towards the girl who had cried out in fear at my appearance. It was a normal reaction, and it wasn't one that should have caused the anger that I could feel roiling off of the man that was almost upon us.

"You should turn away," I warned her softly. "You aren't going to want to see what's about to happen."

She jerked in surprise, her head coming to rest on me as she remembered that I was there. There was an odd play of emotions on her face, but after a moment she slowly nodded and turned her back to the doorway. Kneeling on the floor, she placed her hands over her ears as well. Smart girl.

And trusting, something that worried me. I was a virtual stranger, and she had listened without argument. Whether that was because she believed me, or it was conditioned, I didn't know. But I didn't like it.

"Who made that noise?" A man's voice bellowed as he stormed around the corner and into the kitchen.

His eyes were focused on the kneeling, trembling girl a few feet away. He didn't see me as a sick smile spread across his face, his evil intentions clearly written in his eyes.

I stepped up behind him as he paused a few feet inside the doorway to admire his prey. There was a sense of satisfaction mixed in with his anger at being interrupted, and there was a part of me that was glad for what was about to happen.

"That was me," I said in his ear, just soft enough that I could see chill bumps appear on his skin.

Before he could turn to see my face, I grabbed his forehead and tilted his head back. His hands started to glow with magic, the amount of power enough that it would have done some damage, if I had given him the time to use it before I pulled my blade across his throat. My hand tingled and burned where our skin touched, but I had to get close enough to finish the job.

Blood sprayed from his throat as his magic faded, but the red splatter didn't go more than a few feet as the air in front of him solidified, a gurgle escaping him as his legs gave out.

The man wasn't much more than a human wizard, so I didn't have to worry about him healing the wound before it would kill him. Still, I set his body aflame just to be sure. The heat was intense in the closed off space of the kitchen, hot enough to cause images to appear in the air, but a thin layer of solidified air kept anything but the man and his body fluids from burning to ash.

It was the easiest way to dispose of a body, and I used a gentle breeze to clear away the ashes and sweep them out of a crack in the window.

As soon as the body and all the ash were gone, I moved over to the girl, her neck was a bit red from the heat, but it wouldn't be much worse than a burn one would have receive from staying out in the sun for too long.

Laying my hand gently on her shoulder, she jumped with fear, huddling further into herself with her head almost pressed to the floor. I just followed her movement and let my hand stay lightly resting there, sending a cooling sensation to her back until she eventual convinced herself that she wasn't in immediate danger.

Pulling her hands from her ears, she slowly looked at me, though she couldn't see my face from under my hood. Her eyes searched like she wanted to, something I wouldn't allow.

"Wait until tomorrow afternoon, then you can go and report that your master's gone missing. I'll open the safe before I leave, that should give you time to take what you need before anyone comes to investigate his disappearance." I said softly.

She shakily nodded, but her eyes weren't seeing me. Instead she was looking past me over her shoulder like she expected the man to come after her at any moment. It was a feeling that I knew would take years to fade, but those were years that she now had.

"You can make sure that the other women are also taken care of," I said when she continued to stare at the doorway with fear filled eyes.

After a few more moments of silence, I finally stood and stepped towards the same doorway that he had used moments before. I only made it a few steps before the girl got to her feet and ran after me. Her hand grabbing the fabric of my cloak and I paused as she looked slightly down at me. She seemed just as surprised by her own actions as she was the fact that I was smaller than her.

"He's really gone?" Her question was fearful and hopeful at once.

It was something else I knew would take time to feel real. The sensation of eyes always watching. That one false move would bring him coming to deliver a punishment.

"Yes, he's really gone," I agreed with a slight nod. "Your more than welcome to come with me if you wish to see that he isn't here for yourself."

She bit her lip, not sure as her gaze once again made its way to the hallway I was planning to move toward. I waited patiently, thought the ticking of a clock was ever present in the back of my mind. Eventually she gave me a shaky nod, fear still filling her as we started to make our way towards the man's office. Her grip on my cloak tightened and I knew that she wasn't going to release me for a while yet.

My gaze moved to the window, knowing that it hadn't taken much time at all for me to take care of my mark, but still fearing that I was taking too long to make it to the Prince. Fearing that I wouldn't get there before the other assassins did.

The man of the house didn't leap out at us, and I could almost hear the fearful pounding of the young woman's heart as we stepped through the door to his office. He wasn't here, and I felt a small shift in the woman behind me, some of her fear shifting to hope. She still wasn't sure whether or not to believe me, but she had known he was in the house, and now he wasn't.

Moving over to the safe, I used my magic to figure out how to get it open without looking like I was breaking in. That would make the investigators suspicious, and I wasn't going to go through all this trouble just to have the girls I was trying to protect take the fall for a murder they didn't commit.

"How did you do it?" She softly asked, making me pause as I finally got the safe opened. "No offense, but you're not very big, and the master was..."

She let her voice trail off, and I could understand what she was getting at. It was true that I wasn't very big or intimidating, something that my own people had felt the need to comment on often when I was still with them. But that didn't mean that I wasn't strong, and her master and many other men had found that out the hard way.

I found that other women were much more wary of me and my size, something I think had to do with the fact that they understood that size and gender didn't mean anything when it came to causing pain. I had used that to my advantage more than once.

"I took him by surprise," I told her, a partial truth.

She nodded, not asking anymore questions. She didn't really care how I had done it, she just wanted to believe that I had.

"The safe is open, I suggest that you take the money and other goods sooner rather than later in case someone were to discover his disappearance before you can go to the inspector."

"Okay," she agreed.

"And remember," I said, turning to face her and having to look up a bit to see her face. "Wait until tomorrow morning to go, that gives you enough time to plan, but it also makes it seem like he just didn't come home after a night out."

"He does like to stay out over night, but he is almost always home before lunch," she agreed, nodding again.

I knew that, it's why I suggest that time frame in the first place. Just because I hadn't been able to kill him without being ordered to do so didn't mean I hadn't watched him and stopped what I could. He had seen many unfortunate *accidents*, and I wouldn't have stopped until I found a way for one of those accidents to kill him. This just made things easier on me.

"I'm leaving now, but you don't have to fear that man any longer," I told her, watching as her face pinched.

She didn't believe me yet, but she would, and she would be much happier after tonight.

"Thank you," she said, and though I knew she wasn't sure whether to believe me or not, her thanks were heartfelt.

With a nod of my own, I walked over to the window and pushed it open, looking down onto the people below as I leaned over. Pulling on my cloaking spell, and ignoring the gasp behind me, I leapt out as soon as the way below me was clear.

I ran through the streets, weaving between the people that were walking and selling their wares, making my way towards the castle. My chest felt warmer, something in my heart telling me I had done a good thing, even if I had killed someone to do it.

Now, wasn't *that* something.

I was once again sitting on the wall outside the castle, waiting for the other assassins to show up. My research had determined this to be the best spot to enter the grounds without being seen. I only hoped the others weren't stupid enough to try for a different spot, or this was going to get more complicated that I liked.

Footsteps crunching through the leaves of the forest in front of me rang out as the sounds of people approaching reached my ears. Relief filled me, and I hadn't realized how tense I had become while I waited until my shoulders relaxed.

"What are you doing here?" A harsh and husky female voice rang out in front of me.

Tash and her team stepped out of the forest, and I pulled one of my feet up to the wall in front of me, the other dangling over the edge. It was a move designed to give me freedom of movement, but also to disarm my opponents and make them think I was relaxed.

"I was told to come and make sure you didn't screw this up," I said, making up the lie on the spot.

One of the men snickered, I wasn't sure of his name, but he had a reputation for being particularly vicious. As well as trying to get into Tash's pants.

"That's rich coming from you. Aren't you the one who screwed up the first time? Why would he send someone who had already messed up once to make sure that the job got done?" His voice was sarcastic and cruel, but it didn't affect me the way he was hoping.

"He wouldn't," the second man said.

He was quiet, not known for speaking much. But what he did say others listened to. He was also the brains of the group. The others looked at him before their gazes came back to rest on me. They didn't doubt his response at all, which meant that now they were suspicious of my reasoning for being here.

An odd noise came from behind me inside the walls, but I ignored it for the moment, not feeling threatened by whoever was approaching. Not that they would be able to see me. I was only allowing myself to be visible to those in front of me for the moment.

A slow, unkind smile filled my face, even though they wouldn't be able to see it. I shrugged, as I tensed my muscles, ready to move at a moment's notice.

"Guess you got me," I said, my voice more viscous than normal as my magic came to the forefront, and the tension in the air rose to match. "But now that you know, I'm going to have to kill you."

"Traitor!" The first man screamed as I launched myself at them.

The second man stepped in front of the first, his blade raised to clashed with my own instead of his teammate's throat. I pressed a foot to his chest and jumped back to avoid his swing. He flew back into the friend he had just saved, and I twisted my body to avoid the blow Tash was directing at my kidneys. She was a wolf shifter, and her hits would pack a punch if they landed, so it would be best to avoid them all together.

The vicious one that had spoken first was a half vampire, and while he was faster and stronger than a human, he wasn't anywhere near a full vampire's levels. The second man was an unknown to me, though he had always felt cold like stone. His magic and aura giving off a feeling that made me think of reptiles.

All three of them were standing as I landed, and I moved to put my back to the wall. Getting all three of them in front of me as I tried to work out some semblance of a plan. I knew what the first man and Tash were, but the third man in the group felt like he would be the most dangerous. The problem was that I didn't know what he would be able to do, so I was hesitant to get too close before I could get more information.

I knew about most people in the guild, but aside from the Guild Master and his inner circle, there weren't many people that knew what I was. It was the same way with a few others, including the man before me. The Guild Master's inner circle was comprised of his best people, and they knew things that the rest of us didn't. But they also knew better than to gossip with the others about what they knew.

Tash came at me again, her attack fast and vicious. I turned to avoid her at the same time I threw one of my knives at the first man, cursing when it went a bit wide. He cried out in pain, but the blade only lodged itself in his shoulder, not hitting anything vital.

Cursing, I wasn't able to try again as Tash and the second man both came for me at the same time. They sent off a flurry of blows that I was able to dodge, but I wasn't able to fight back against them while also watching the third man pull out his short sword. He was good with a blade, and he seemed to favor them, but I hadn't ever seen the other two with any kind of weapon.

Tash usually shifted to take someone out, and the fact that she hadn't yet meant that either they had a plan, or she didn't consider me a threat.

"Why are you here if you weren't sent by the Guild Master?" The second man asked as he backed off just in time for the first to swing at me with the sword.

I was barely able to dodge the swing as Tash was behind me, stopping me from moving back any further.

"Is it because of your *morals* that you're here? Did you even try to kill him when you failed before?" The man said as he continued stepping back, his hair seemed to blow in the breeze, though the movements were off.

The magic around him seemed to get stronger, the feeling heavy in the air and my tension got worse. What was he about to do? And how did I stop fighting the others long enough to stop him from succeeding?

"What does it matter?" I asked him.

"It doesn't," he said with a shrug, and I watched as his skin took on a pale grey color, his hair grouping together in thicker strands as he eyes seemed to glow green. "I just wanted to know before I killed you."

His hair continued to move as I dodged the other two, and I managed to drive one of my blades deep into the half vampire's inner thigh, hitting the vein I knew would cause him to bleed out within minutes. The half vampire backed away from me as he called out with anger and pain. Then, like an idiot, he pulled the blade free, allowing the blood to run more freely from his body.

"Idiot," Tash snarled, her face starting to shift as she watched her teammates life slowly drain out of him.

I pulled out one of my enchanted weapons, something that looked like a stick. It grew as the symbols on it started to glow with my magic and a sharp tip formed on the end, the spear materializing in less than a second.

It was too late for Tash to stop her shift, and I took the opening that was before me, driving the weapon upwards into her stomach and into her heart, watching as she choked on her own blood before the life could leave her eyes. Her hands grasped my arm, failing to break through my cloak in a last attempt to wound me.

A snarl sounded out from the third man as his second teammate fell at my feet. As I looked him over, I felt a bit of fear start to fill my chest, realization dawning on me. His skin looked like stone, but his hair continued to move on its own, and I realized it was because it wasn't hair at all, but a group of snakes.

He was a gorgon, and though I hadn't thought it possible for a man to be a gorgon, I couldn't deny the proof in front of me.

It was supposed to be a trait that was only passed down through the female line, but that was a thought for another time. Looking away from him before I could meet his eyes, this fight had just gotten a lot harder. And there was a part of me that was thrilled by that fact.

He lunged at me, and I was barely able to block the blow in time. If I couldn't read his body movements to predict his moves, then I was going to have to work harder to defend myself and look for an opening. If I looked him in the eyes, or even looked towards him for too long I would be turned to stone.

While I wasn't sure I would stay that way forever, the process would be painful, and it would give him time to finish his mission and make his way back to the guild. He could also choose to kill me if he didn't tell the Guild Master of my betrayal first.

Neither option was good, and I couldn't allow for them to happen.

The fight continued on, but he was able to get in a few hits on me this time. And with the stone-like quality to his skin, the blows hurt a lot more than before. Despite the fact that I couldn't look at him directly, the fight wasn't getting us anywhere. I had to end it soon.

We both jerked back in surprise when a blade appeared on the ground between us, and I looked up at the newest threat, not having heard anyone coming. The Prince and his two companions were sitting on the wall above us, the knight holding another blade in his hand lazily.

"What are you doing here?" The Prince asked, sounding bored.

I wasn't sure if he was talking to me, or the man I was fighting, but neither of us spoke up. I could feel the gaze of the assassin on my face, but I avoided both his gaze and the gaze of those above me.

"He didn't know you were here?" The assassin before me asked.

His voice was a mix of confusion, disbelief, and laughter. But he didn't wait for an answer before he lunged for me.

I barely avoided the blade that had suddenly appeared in his hand, too distracted by the men's appearance behind me to dodge it completely. He managed to get a shallow cut to my arm, but when he kept going, I knew he was now aiming for the Prince.

Taking the opening he had given me, I pulled a weapon that turned into a longer version of a sword, swinging towards the back of his neck.

The blade sliced cleanly through just as he let his own blade fly. I watched, torn between stopping it and not wanting to get within range of the Prince and his men.

I shouldn't have worried though, the blade bounced off a magical barrier that was a foot in front of the three men. Then it fell to the ground before the now dead man who had thrown it, and I looked between the blade and the men above me. Then, I looked at the other bodies around me.

"Would you like to explain what happened and what you're doing here?" Merrick asked me.

"No, I'm good." I said, giving them a small wave as I started to back away.

"You're an odd one, Kitten," the Prince said, and something

both warm and sharp ran through me.

"Yes, I know," I agreed.

Then, before they could say anything else, I turned and ran into the forest.

I heard them leap down from the wall, but I wasn't interested in getting caught like the first time, and I was in a much better position than before. Using the speed of my people, I ran through the woods faster than the eye could see as I used the trees to my advantage.

They didn't catch up, and before long I knew it was safe to slow down.

I was heading back towards the guild, even though I didn't want to. I couldn't be around when it was made known that the assassins sent after the Prince had failed once again. I just hoped that the Prince didn't tell anyone that it was me that had killed them.

That would mean my death. And I was pretty sure that my time was already running out.

CHAPTER SIX

THINGS HAD BEEN GOING TOO SMOOTHLY. Much too good for *me*; I should have known better. Three weeks had gone by since the last mission meant to kill me, and I knew I should have looked before taking this assignment. I should have known there was something hinky about the smile the Guild Master had sent me, more than just the fact that he wanted me gone.

My new assignment was Xavier, the head guard and companion of the one and only Crown Prince Adair.

When the other three assassins sent for the Prince had failed to return back, a scout had been sent out to find out what had happened. He had returned that same night to report back that they had all been taken out, and that the Prince and his men had been the ones to do it.

A weight had been lifted from my shoulders at the news, but I should have known it was the calm before the storm.

This new assignment had a strange mix of emotions running through me. Something in my chest relaxed when I knew it shouldn't have. A calmness had settled inside me when I saw his name and information listed on my parchment. If he was the target, that meant he was alive. And if he was alive, then that meant there was a reason someone wanted him dead. And the only reason I could surmise would be due to his position in the court. And that meant that all *three* of the men I had met were alive and well.

Something about the bond I had seen between the three led me to believe that he would have stepped down if the Prince were dead.

It was just a guess; I didn't know them as people. But I hadn't been wrong yet, and I didn't think I was in this case, either.

Biting my lip, I debated about what I should do. There was no way that I was going to be able to kill him. It wasn't that I doubted my skill, though I didn't think I could take all three on at the same time, it was that I knew he wasn't a horrible person. And I doubted very much that he had become a bad person in the past few weeks.

It was the same predicament I had faced a few months ago, and even last night. I had nowhere to go, and nothing else in my life that I could do. The guild would come after me if I defected, and there wasn't anywhere I could hide from them. I was good, but no one could stay on guard every hour of everyday. It wasn't possible. I would mess up at some point, and that would be the moment someone came to take me down.

So, I had two options: I could run, from the assignment *and* the guild, or I could go and warn them again that there was a price on their heads and hope that they would at least end my life quickly. The guild wouldn't be quite so nice.

Neither option was a good one, and I didn't relish the thought of dying so soon now that something inside me seemed to want to live, but it was bound to happen eventually.

Another thought came to mind, and something in me settled as a smile tilted up the corner of my lips.

The Guild Master was assuming, after my last failure, that I would either run or chance failing once more. I knew it and he knew it. But I knew he thought that the fear of turning on the guild was enough to make most people hesitate. But if he was boxing me into a corner that was going to kill me anyway, why not go out revealing all his secrets?

I wasn't stupid, and he knew that, so I wasn't sure why he hadn't just killed me instead of toying with me.

Though, I didn't know what had caused him to seek my death in the first place, I wasn't going to sit and wait for him to find a way to do it. Not when, after rebuilding that man's shop a few months ago, I finally felt like I was starting to *live* for the first time. I may not have understood what it meant to help instead of hurt at the time, what it meant to help others, but I did now. And I *liked* it.

I enjoyed the thrill of knowing that I was able to help. It was even better that they never learned what or who I was. Something inside me enjoyed being an unknown helper.

Path decided, I slowly wandered out of the guild hall and through the forest. There wasn't a point in rushing. There was no great hurry for me to kill a man that I knew I wouldn't be able to hurt.

It was too bad life had turned out this way. From our brief interactions I had a feeling that me and those men would have been gotten along just fine in a different life.

All of them had a sense of humor that I could appreciate. Their personalities not clashing with my own in our brief interactions.

There wasn't a lot of laughter in my life, more fear and sorrow than anything. But I enjoyed those brief glances of happiness and laughter I got around those that I wasn't there to kill. Maybe some of them would remember me fondly once I was gone.

That was all I could ask for, at the end of the day.

I was sitting on the wall, in the same spot as the first time I had come here. It was becoming a habit of mine. But this time I had a different target in mind, even if it was almost exactly the same situation as the first time I had come here. Aside from a few more patrols, some of which were obviously just fresh from the training fields, nothing seemed different.

The sun was just starting to set as I watched the castle. There was a bit more activity that before, but nothing that made me think anything big was about to go down. They were probably planning a party of some sort, but there hadn't been any whispers on the wind about it. That in and of itself was odd, but I wasn't too worried.

I was planning on being long gone before then.

A new plan had formed while I had walked here, and I was hoping it would work. I would use this opportunity to fake my own death. There was enough reason to believe I would die here, the first and only mission I had ever failed had happened in this exact spot, after all.

The problem was finding a body that was close enough to mine to be a good substitute. I wasn't against killing someone to get it, but I wasn't going to take the life of an innocent just to try and save my own skin.

As soon as the sun was gone from the sky, I let myself drop from the wall to the ground. My cloaking spell was firmly in place, and even movement wouldn't affect it this time. My hood was up and covering my face just like always, but the spells had been reinforced. The less people who knew what I looked like, the less likely it was that my faked death would be discovered.

When I got to the castle, I didn't bother climbing the wall and instead I just walked in the back door. There was enough activity going on that I wasn't worried it would be noticed if the door opened and shut with no one appearing.

Making my way down the halls, I still did my best to take the least used walkways, not wanting to chance bumping into someone. While my spell would keep me out of sight of others, it did nothing to stop them from feeling me if we were to bump into each other. After the wolf issue I had on a recent mission, I was also blocking my scent. There was no reason to give the shifters an advantage that they didn't need.

People were talking both excited and fearfully about a guest that was coming to the castle for dinner, but no names were said, and I wasn't able to glean any more information about who this visitor could be.

The new presence could complicate things, but I wasn't going to let it stop me from accomplishing my mission.

Walking faster, I made my way to the rooms I knew would hold the knight. Him, the Prince, and the Prince's advisor were all in the same hall of rooms. It made figuring out a path much simpler, but it also meant that there was a chance all three of them would be together.

While I already had multiple escape routes planned, I didn't want to have to hurt myself escaping again.

Arriving outside the door I knew to be his, I pressed my ear against it to listen. When no sounds came from inside, I opened the door and peered in. There was no one inside the small common area, and no noise came from inside the bed chamber either.

He wasn't here.

Pushing into the room, I walked across it and pushed the already open window wider and settled myself on the ledge to wait. There was no telling how long it would take for him to arrive, but I would wait here until I could warn him.

Night fell, and I heard the sounds of activity slowly start to fade until everyone but the necessary staff were getting ready for bed.

Finally, after hours of listening for him, I heard the sound of footsteps heading this way.

"Do you think she'll come?" Xavier asked as he swung his door open.

"Yes, but we can't expect it to be soon," Merrick said as all three of the men walked into the room. "You know she was busy last night; she'll need to rest up."

My curiosity peaked as I wondered who they were talking about, the other was left to figure out what to do now that all three of them were here. My back was to the window, so getting cornered inside the room wasn't a concern, but getting off the grounds before one of them could call out *was*.

"I bet she comes sooner rather than later," Xavier said as the other two joined him sitting on the little couch set up. "Want to make a wager on it?"

While I was curious about who they were talking about, I didn't have much time if I wanted to enact my plan. I still needed to find a body to replace my own, and I needed to do it soon.

"And while you're wagering on that, you can also bet on who will be the next one to have a price put on their head." I said dryly, amused with them.

All three of them jumped to their feet, the Prince's face a snarl as he looked at where I was sitting. His eyes flared a bright, gold color as he looked at where I was now visible. Then they faded back to their original green when he saw it was me.

Interesting.

"Well, now there's no point in wagering at all," Xavier muttered petulantly.

Confusion flew through my head before I remembered the reason I was here.

"You guys really should learn not to piss so many people off," I told them, tensing my muscles in preparation for my departure. "Now, it's not just the Prince that the guild is after."

They all looked at each other and I got ready to make my exit, my muscles tensed and ready.

"Be ready, knight," I told him, meeting his eyes from under my hood as Merrick lifted his hands to gesture. "Once tonight is over, they're going to send someone else, and more people are going to try to accept the contracts with both you and the Prince on the list. Seems you guys are worth a pretty penny."

Merrick grunted in frustration when his spell hit my wall of air. There was a brief flare as magic ran over the surface of my air magic with a flurry of pretty colors.

"Fool me once, mage," I wagged a gloved finger at him. "Watch your backs."

With my last words, I threw myself backwards out the window, twisting and bouncing into a roll when I hit the ground. I was up and running towards the wall before they could even get to the window.

An unsettled feeling came over me, and I slowed as I got closer to the wall. All three men were watching, but none of them had called out to the patrols that were wandering around.

The closer I got to the wall, the more I became sure that something else was in play here.

When I got to the wall it was to find that there was a spell designed to trap me in place. I stared up at the top of the large, brick monstrosity, and debated how best to handle it. The spell trap ran the length of the wall, but I didn't know how high up it went.

Taking a chance, I skipped the climbing portion and leapt up and over, using a bit of solidified air as a step when I got to the top instead of touching the wall itself. I could feel the pull of the spell as it tried to grab me, but I wasn't going to let it pull me in. Landing on the other side, I started to run towards the trees.

There was no sign of pursuit, but I didn't slow down. The feeling of unease growing the longer I ran without pursuit.

I was so busy looking for magical traps as I ran, that when a regular snare came into view it was too late to stop. I twisted barely avoiding it, only to step right into a second, better hidden one. There was a snap as the rope closed over my ankle, the sound of both the rope closing and my ankle breaking happening at once.

A surprised sound of pain escaped me, and I lunged up at the rope, trying to take some of the weight off my now broken ankle. My face paled and I started to pant when the unexpected pain stole the breath from my lungs. Pulling a knife, I tried to cut through the rope, knowing even as I did, that I wouldn't be able to counteract the spells that had snapped to life without being able to concentrate. I was curled awkwardly as I tried to bend to take the weight off my leg.

Pulling myself hand over hand, I slowly got myself so that my leg was below me instead of above my head, and the throbbing seemed to get worse all at once. Adrenaline was still running through me from being taken by surprise, and I kept going until the rope was dangling below me and I was to the branch that it was tied to.

When I tried to grab the branch to pull myself up though, it burned me. Not in the way that fire did, but like acid scalding my skin. I let go of it instantly on instinct and had to grab at the rope when I started to fall. My skin burned as the rope rubbed and heated up even through my gloves. I was barely able to stop myself as my ankle twisted at another funny angle, and a grunt of pain escaped.

I was effectively trapped until someone came or I could get myself out of this.

It wasn't that pain was unfamiliar, but this time it had been unexpected, and I hadn't been able to brace myself against it. My fear and panic had only made it worse. So, first things first, I had to get my breathing and emotions under control. I needed to think of a way out of this before someone came to collect me. None of which would be possible if I panicked.

I took a deep breath and held it, releasing it slowly as I re-centered myself. Continuing the exercise until I was calm enough to think through my situation. I would create a list of things to try, and go through them all one by one until I was free.

I was supposed to fake my death, not actually *die*, and like an animal at that. Though, it was probably the least I deserved.

I would figure out a way to free myself.

I   had   to.

CHAPTER SEVEN

IT DIDN'T WORK.

Nothing worked.

Not fire, not a blade, not any of the spells I knew. Nothing had helped me get free, and the sun was on the horizon.

My foot and ankle were numb right now, but that was only because I hadn't moved either for the last few hours. I could see how bad the swelling was, but I was too scared to take a closer look at it right now. My arms were shaking and my shoulders were screaming with a different sort of pain. Holding myself in the same position for hours had made the muscles rebel against me. They wanted to move, but I wasn't going to put pressure on my ankle if I didn't have to. Not yet.

The sound of steps in the leaves came to me, and I turned in the direction that I heard them coming from, not knowing what to expect.

The Prince didn't make noise when he moved, and neither did his companions.

"Finally," Xavier said as the three men I was both dreading and hoping would show came into view.

I silently watched as they got closer, relief filling me even as I didn't know what to expect. They were the reason I was hanging here, but they would also be the only way I could get free of this trap.

"It's not like we could skip any of the traps," Merrick said. "We weren't sure which way she would go. And there was always the chance that she would have been able to avoid them all."

"With how many you set it was doubtful," the Prince said.

His eyes ran over my shaking form, something flashing through his eyes when they landed on my swollen ankle.

I kept silent, not wanting to make my situation worse. I just wanted them to let me down. Then I could take stock of the situation and make a plan.

"Get her down. Now."

Adair's voice was demanding for the first time since I had met him, and it made my muscles clench with tension.

"Okay," the mage said, the spell on the rope fading with a gesture of his hand.

I didn't wait for them to do anything else, instead I brough up my own blade and severed the now magicless rope. My body dropped, pain flaring from my ankle as I shifted it so that I wouldn't land on it as I hit the ground. But after so long in the same position, and not having any strength left, my butt was the next thing to hit the ground.

It sent reverberations through my legs and took my breath away. While I had been able to stay calm, I hadn't been able to block the pain out completely. Instead of getting up and running like I wanted to, I bent my head down and just tried to breathe through the wave of pain that was rushing through me.

A warm hand came down to rest on the back on my neck through my cloak, and I tensed, not sure what was about to happen.

"I'm sorry," the Prince said softly, something about his voice soothing my ruffled feathers. "We didn't mean to hurt you. We just wanted to stop you."

"I'm fine," my voice croaked, the lie obvious, even to me.

"Shit," Xavier said moving to kneel beside us and causing me to tense up again. "What can we do?"

I snorted out a breath of a laugh and all three of them looking at me as I looked up at the knight. "Isn't your job to defend and take care of the Prince? Does that not include the basics of injury care in battle?"

It probably shouldn't have been funny to me, but it was amusing to see that he had forgotten the basic skills required of his station. I knew that most of the soldiers in this kingdom were taught basic aid skills as a requirement, it was something that others sneered at. But I thought it was smart. You never knew when you may need those skills to treat others, or yourself.

"Right," he agreed, nodding as he reached out to me.

I moved back, wincing as my leg dragged on the ground, and stopped when I felt heat at my back. I held up a hand to stop him from getting closer.

"That doesn't mean I want you to touch me." I told him.

The Prince's hand fell away from me as I moved, taking the warmth of his hand with him. I knew I shouldn't be here. Not now. Broken ankle or not, I needed to leave. My plan was getting further and further from reach the longer I stayed here, and I didn't have much time left.

"Don't run," Merrick said as he leaned over all of us. "I don't want to have to hold you here by force."

He seemed sincere in not wanting to hold me, but I didn't like to be threatened at all.

I bristled, wanting to run just because he told me not to. The Prince reached out and grabbed my leg at the knee, stopping me from both running and keeping my leg from being bumped as I tried to move again.

"You're only making it worse," he chastised me. "Stop moving until we can stabilize your ankle."

Not seeing anything else I *could* do, I pursed my lips and settled down.

"Yes, Your Highness," I taunted, doing what he asked but letting him know that I wasn't happy about it.

He snorted with humor, and I could have sworn there was a curl of smoke that came out of his nostrils.

"You aren't too bright, are you?" The advisor said with humor. "Smarting off to a Prince like that."

I shrugged, not offended that he thought me unintelligent. I could use that to my advantage later if I got the chance. But it also sounded like he was making fun of me more than actually calling me stupid, so that probably wasn't a real option.

"I figure I already have a death sentence on my head, so there's no use pandering to those around me to stop something guaranteed to happen."

Xavier grabbed my leg near my ankle and the pain made the blood rush through my head. The sound blocking out whatever response I was given. The pain was intense, and I fought the urge to stab at the people around me that were making it spike.

"Settle down, Kitten," the Prince said as he set his hand once again on the back of my cloaked neck.

The urge to show this man my claws was strong. But his hand was a soothing warmth, and mixed with his voice I could swear the pain was dulling the longer he was here. The knight looked at my ankle, pulling at the leg of my pants and making me release a grunt of pain as he was finally able to pull it up above the swelling.

I wasn't sure why I wasn't fighting them harder, or at all. I was letting these strangers be here when I was vulnerable, and it went against everything I had been taught. Everything I was. It didn't matter that I assumed getting caught was a death sentence, I should have fought harder.

"Merrick," Xavier said softly, bringing me back to the present, and allowing me to figure out what was happening.

"Stop it," I slurred at the mage.

He was using magic to keep me calm and still. That mixed with the Prince's potent presence, and I was like putty on the ground. Useless goo.

"No," Merrick said, far too happy, if you asked me; which he hadn't.

"But I need to...need to..." my voice trailed off as Xavier touched my ankle and my mind clouded over.

My eyes were drifting shut, and the spell he was weaving over me felt like a warm blanket that I couldn't push off.

"Please..." I muttered softly, knowing that my chances of living without the guild hunting me were dying as I grew closer to sleep.

They all seemed to pause at that. Whether it was because it was so unexpected, or something else, I didn't know, but they didn't stop. None of them bothered to ask me anything at all.

Instead, they just continued what they were doing, and despite my best efforts, my eyes closed as sleep came for me.

For the second time since I had met them, I had failed my job, and was put to sleep by the mage's spell.

I woke in the same bed as before, but instead of immediately getting up and trying to run, I just laid there and stared up at the ceiling.

I had failed at killing the Prince and his knight. I had failed to fake my own death. I had failed to run.

Now there was no chance of pretending I had died with my failure.

The fact that I hadn't killed them would get back to the guild, that much was true enough. But if they found out that I was captured, and not dead, that would spark worry in the Guild Master. While I knew assumed the fear of his ability and the pain he could cause was enough to stop people from talking, there was always the chance that someone else's torture could be worse, and secrets would be spilled.

There wasn't much I could do but wait for which ever assassins he would send to gather me or kill me outright. He would be sending more than one, the fact that I was the best solo player in the guild was reason enough to do so. It would heighten his chances for success.

But there wasn't a guarantee that the Prince wouldn't kill me first, and now that my plan had gone out the window, I would stick to my original plan. I would tell them everything I knew about the guild and its players. About the master himself, and what I knew of his weaknesses.

They would know everything that I did before the night was out, and then I would happily walk to my death, a smile on my face as the rope encircled my throat.

Knowing better than to try and escape, I sat up in the bed, realizing for the first time as I did so that my ankle didn't hurt at all. Then, an entirely new fear took hold.

Slowly, and with shaking hands, I reached up, confirming what I had just now realized.

My hood was down, and my cloak was gone. They had seen my face, had seen who I was. There was no chance of escaping from them now.

Panic flared as I looked around, spotting my garment hanging from a chair across the room. I jerked myself to my feet, bracing for a pain that never came as I ran and grabbed it. Pulling it around me as fast as I could, some of my anxiety faded as it settled on my shoulders. The pull of the fabric a familiar weight that meant nothing in the face of them knowing what I was. And what I looked like.

They had seen my face; they would be able to describe me to anyone they chose to. There would be nowhere I could go to escape. It had always been my hope that I would be able to take care of those who knew what I looked like and live a life free from threat when I was strong enough. Now that hope was gone, shattered as it lay at my feet.

It was irrational. I was planning to die after giving away secrets better left hidden, but the fear was so engrained that I couldn't help it.

My ankle was better, though there was still a small remnant of pain. The bone was whole, and I wasn't one hundred percent sure how that was possible. I would have healed much faster than a human, but my body couldn't heal *that* fast.

Putting that out of my mind for now, I bent over the desk the chair was placed in front of and started to go through the items contained inside. Like the first time I had woken up here, all my weapons were still on me, so I wasn't worried about defending myself. Instead, I looked for something to write on.

There was a full drawer of parchment, as well as a writing utensil, and with the needed items gathered I sat at the desk and started to write.

It may not have made much sense to anyone else, but I knew there was a chance that someone had been sent out almost immediately after I had left. There was a chance that my potential killer was here, even now, lurking and waiting for a chance to take my life. I couldn't wait until I next saw the Prince to tell him what I knew. There was also a chance that my killer would take the opportunity to kill him and the knight at the same time.

There were a lot of people that didn't care about collateral damage, which meant the mage was also in danger. Four for the price of one. A lot of the others in the guild were there by choice, and that meant that they didn't have a strong moral compass. They would take any job that paid well, no matter who they hurt in the process.

So, instead of saying anything that could be overheard by the wrong people and risking the three men's lives further, I wrote it all down. Everything that I knew, everything that I had gathered or guessed at. All my theories and information was written down until there were enough pages to fill a book and my hand was cramped up with pain.

"Of all the places we expected to find you, your room wasn't on the list," the Prince said, amused.

"I do like to have the element of surprise on my side," I said, the words coming out before I could filter them.

"I assume that would be a good thing in your line of work," Merrick said, none of the expected hate or judgement in his tone that I was expecting.

"Mhm," I hummed in agreement, finally turning to look at them.

The papers were in a neat stack on the desk, enchanted so that only the three men standing in the doorway, or someone that they all trusted exclusively, could read them. There was no need to show them now though, they would see them soon enough. Another wave of my hand made sure that they would stay safe and out of the wrong hands. You could never be too careful.

"How can I help you?" I asked leaning back in the chair, waiting to see what they were here for.

If they were here to take me to my death, I wouldn't fight them. Even if I wasn't ready to die, between them and the guild, I wasn't sure I had much of a choice in the matter.

I had come to terms with death a long time ago. I had been forced to accept that it was going to happen from a young age. You weren't raised around a bunch of death dealers expecting to live a long, happy, healthy life. Death was a part of everyday life; it was all I knew. And it wasn't only the assassins that had made it clear that was what I should expect.

"Why didn't you try to run again?" The Prince asked, ignoring my question.

"What would have been the point? My plan was already ruined." I told him with a shrug. "The death you have in store is going to be much kinder than the one the guild is planning; I can guarantee that."

His face changed as the others also seemed surprised by my words.

"That's—"

Whatever Xavier was about to say was cut off as another man, this one in light armor, came rushing up to them.

"Your Highness, the patrol just saw some intruders enter the grounds near the garden. What would you like them to do?" The young kid was out of breath, and almost seemed excited at the potential to see some action.

"So, it's begun," I whispered under my breath, standing, and producing a knife in each hand.

"I'll take care of them and then we can continue our conversation," I told the Prince, not looking at him as I pushed past all four men and made my way towards the garden.

There were a few people that called out in surprise as I didn't bother to cloak myself, and one of the maids even went as far as to dramatically throw herself into the wall as I passed. I chuckled darkly, pushing down the urge to lunge at her and growl. But I didn't think that would be taken kindly by the men behind me.

Now wasn't the time, and that wasn't the kind thing to do anyway.

"Can I come too, Your Highness?" The boy asked, though it wasn't more than a whisper.

The Prince shouldn't have been coming at all, and I wondered why the young man wanted to tag along. This wasn't something that was going to be pleasant. But at the same time, maybe they were all hoping that I would die, and they could watch me do it.

I picked up the pace a little as I felt the grimy energy of the men who were here, my cloak billowing out around me dramatically and making me want to laugh at my own dramatics. There was nothing about this situation that was funny, but that was a part of the reason I wanted to laugh.

The men were waiting for me, surrounded by guards that they weren't even trying to attack. They had their orders, and they were sure that they would win the fight that was about to happen. But I wasn't going back to the guild, and I had no more reason to fear letting myself fight. The Guild Master couldn't use me anymore, I was one fight away from a death sentence, and there was no more reason to hold back.

Magic started to gather inside my body, the energy swirling all throughout me with relish. A sigh of relief escaped me when I stopped blocking my abilities for the first time since I was a child.

A warm presence stepped up on one side of me, and I didn't have to look to know who it was. Merrick stepped up to my other side, and Xavier was at my back. If I didn't know better, I would have thought they were protecting me.

But I *did* know better.

It was the first time I had allowed myself to be surrounded, and with them all standing so close I realized how tall they were for the first time. Objectively, I knew they were all taller than me, but I hadn't realized just how much until I was surrounded by them.

Though I knew it shouldn't have, being in the center of this death march made me more confident about the upcoming fight. I was going to win. And they would make sure there was no collateral damage.

The thought flashed through my mind once more that if the situation were different, we would have made a good team. It floated through my head like a false promise, but this situation wasn't different.

I was an assassin with a price on her head, and they were well-liked royalty.

All time for thoughts of friends had passed; I needed to get my head in the game.

We walked out of the double doors that lead to the garden

area, and my eyes flicked up to the sun one last time. This fight was only going to end when both of them were dead, there was no   alternative.

CHAPTER EIGHT

"DON'T INTERFERE," I TOLD THE PRINCE QUIETLY.

"Why?" His question was curious, not like he was upset that I was trying to keep him out of the fight.

"Because one of these men can control you if he touches you even once. It doesn't wear off, and it's a bitch to try and fight his influence once he has you bound." I had only managed it because he had almost been dead, and I didn't relish him ever getting that close to me again.

Fear tried to fill me at the things he was capable of, my eye burning, but I needed to focus. So, I used that fear and channeled it into my senses, all of them sharpening to an almost unbearable level.

"As you wish," the Prince said with a nod, taking a deliberate step back. "No one is to interfere in this fight unless she states otherwise, understood?"

My back straightened with surprise as the rest of the men gathered lowered their weapons and chanted: "Yes sir."

I hadn't expected him to listen, or to get the others to step out of this fight. And if the looks on some of the gathered faces were any indication, they hadn't either.

"Take them down quickly, Kitten." The Prince murmured, and I was strangely touched by his words.

"As you wish," I responded with a smile, hearing a small, but deep chuckle come from the big man.

He had said the words with confidence. Like he didn't doubt that I could take them on even though it was clear they were much larger than me. The man that could control people was Brand, and he was related to Brock, the monster who could control the blood of those who were hurt around him. Seeing him left me to wonder if he knew what I had done to his brother. My guess was that he didn't.

There was speculation that Brock had been killed, but no one knew who had done it, or where he had been. When he had followed me, it hadn't been on the Guild Master's orders. He had been assigned a different case nearby that him and his friends hadn't ever finished.

It was a relief to know that the Guild Master didn't know all the details of what had gone on that night, but he still wanted me dead, so the situation wasn't much better.

Looking at the second man, Sar, I felt my nerves grow. While I didn't know him well, his brutality was almost a legend. The Guild Master wanted to make sure that I didn't survive here, and I was going to make sure that I *did*, if only for a while, just to spite him.

"So, it's true," Sar said as he lifted the axe by his side.

The weapon was almost as tall as I was, but it looked like a toy in his hand. He was part troll, and it showed in his height and body mass.

"And what is that?" I asked, making a plan in my head that I knew would go to shit as soon as they moved.

"You really are a traitor to the guild, just like Jyria said you were." Sar's use of the Guild Master's name made me flinch the slightest bit.

I hated that man more than almost anyone else in this world. Yet, a smile still escaped me at Sar's words.

"He knows nothing," I told them, ignoring the shuffling feet of those around me. "He was just spouting nonsense to justify his want to kill me."

They didn't look like they believed a word of what I had just said, but they didn't need to.

"But," I said, my muscles tensing in preparation for the fight. "It *wasn't* a lie."

And with those words I threw my knives at both of them, forcing them to separate from each other as I ran at them faster than the eye could see.

Sar may not have been faster than me, but he was stronger, and without waiting to see where I would attack, he turned and swung his axe at the men that were near him.

Cursing, I ran faster, pulling out another stick looking object that glowed with power as it grew into a staff that was just shorter than I was. Using my magic and strength, I stepped into the path of the blade and braced myself for the impact.

His axe slammed into my staff, not making a dent in the weapon but forcing my feet back before I could stop myself. The men behind me grunted in surprise, moving back out of his reach quickly when I appeared before them.

"You always were a bleeding heart," Brand said from right behind me.

But I had sensed him moving, and I used my cloak to hide

my body as I leaned forward and kicked back at him at the same time. He let out a grunt as the wind left his stomach, and I gripped the axe in front of me, the blade biting into my palms as I pushed down on it and jumped, using Sar's own strength against him as I landed on the blade and drew my twin swords. The blades grew and shifted from two other wands that glowed.

"Check mate," I told the troll as I crossed my arms and drew both blades through his thick neck, severing his head and leaping from his now limp arms to land with a roll a few feet away from his body.

I came to a stop on my feet in a crouch, one leg to the side as I watched the stronger of my two opponents. Quick as a snake, Brand reached out and grabbed one of the Prince's men, the man's eyes going blank as he assumed control.

The others stepped even farther back, but he wasn't looking to take anyone else; he already had all the ammunition he needed.

A growl escaped me, not at all sounding human as I looked at my new complication.

"I'm sorry, Your Highness," I apologized to the Prince.

"I understand," he muttered quietly, his voice resigned.

I snorted because I didn't think that he did. "This may take a bit longer than I had planned."

"You're going to kill the Prince's man?" Brand asked tauntingly.

"Not if I can help it," I muttered quiet enough that he wouldn't hear me.

"You know that there isn't a way to save him, not now that he's mine." His voice was smug, as the other men around us tensed up in preparation to fight for their comrade.

"Isn't there?" I asked him softly, taunting him right back.

His face darkened as he looked at me, knowing I was referring to the time he had taken control of me.

"He isn't like you," Brand snarled. "You're an abomination! You shouldn't have been allowed to live."

There was a snarl from behind me, but all I did was bare my teeth in something similar to a smile. I had been told the same thing all my life. So, while the words hurt, I was able to let them roll off my back.

"While all that may be true," I agreed, causing a spark in the ignorant man's eyes. "The guard has me on his side, and that will be enough."

I ran at both of them, the guards moves stilted as his body tried to adjust to being under someone else control. It would take at least a few minutes for Brand's control to fully settle, and I wanted this to be over long before then.

Using the guard's body as a launch pad, I leapt up and used his shoulder as a step so that I could aim a kick for Brand's face.

The guard fell onto his back, rolling around as his body tried to figure out how to get back up. Brand was barely able to dodge my kick, his reflexes not much slower than mine...at least not when I was playing human.

I forced him to turn his back on the man that was still struggling on the ground, and started to attack him, forcing him to go on the defensive and leading him to the center of the garden.

My attacks started to speed up as I couldn't actually let our skin touch if I wanted to stay in control of my own mind, but I was still able to hit him in any of the places he was covered in cloth. I also had to avoid his blocks, which meant I had to pull my punches and reverse my moves last minute, wasting my strength on this useless activity.

Weapons were out as long as I wanted to save the guard, and that left me at a disadvantage that he was trying to use against me.

The man on the ground, behind me now, was still without Brand being able to focus on him during my flurry of blows. And as soon as my target was standing where I wanted him to, I stopped and stepped back, watching him as he panted for air.

"What are you doing?" He asked suspiciously, the others around us as silent as a tomb.

"What all abominations do," I told him. "I was wondering why someone who knew me would pick a garden as the arena to fight, then I saw Sar and figured it was his idea. He wasn't part of the inner circle."

It was satisfying to see the rest of the smug confidence leave his face to be replaced with fear. His head whipped around from side to side as he finally seemed to realize where we were standing.

Cursing up a storm, he tried to turn like he was going to run, only to find that he was trapped. Vines from the rose bush he was standing right in front of were creeping farther up his body. Leaving bloody cuts where the now longer and sharper thorns were cutting deep into his skin.

He was cursing up a storm in fear and pain as he pulled a blade trying to cut his way free. But the vines were growing too fast and thick for him to make much headway in freeing himself. It wasn't long before both his arms and legs were trapped and pulled away from his body. His knife clattered to the ground as the thorns burrowed into the muscles of his forearms and he was forced to relax his grip.

Securely bound, I turned toward the Prince, knowing what was about to come next wouldn't be pleasant. And for some strange reason I didn't want him to think less of me than he already did.

"I think it would be best if you weren't present for what's about to happen." I told him emotionlessly.

Even though I knew he wouldn't be able to see my face through my cloak, I tried to put as much emphasis in my words as I could.

Something shifted in his face, but I wasn't sure what he was thinking. He turned and looked over the others that were gathered, and the man that had been taken over lying still on the ground. I walked over to him slowly, knowing that Brand could start to control him again at any moment. Though I also knew he was in enough pain that it should have derailed any clear thoughts.

The thorns in the vine were still growing, and every little shift of his body would only cause them to dig deeper still.

When the guard didn't move to attack me, I slowly bent to throw his weight over my shoulder. A grunt escaped as he was heavier than I expected with his armor on, but I didn't need to take him far. Some of the others around us gripped their weapons tighter, and I paused while I waited for them to decide if they were going to attack me or not.

They didn't like me touching their man, but it was tough shit if they wanted to actually have more than a husk of him left over.

"Everyone clear out," the Prince's voice rang out, a small amount of anger on his face when he looked at those in front of me with their weapons at the ready.

Grumbling an unhappy 'Yes sir,' they made sure to give me untrusting and hateful looks before they turned and left the area.

When only the four original men were left standing, I moved closer to Brand and gently laid the guard near him. It seemed like it would be a stupid thing to bring him closer to the man controlling him, but I wasn't sure how close he needed to be for what I was about to do to work. I had been touching the man at the time I broke myself free, and I didn't know if that had helped me, but I wasn't going to take the chance that it did when the guards life was at stake.

The Prince was standing with his friends to the side of us, and one of the Guild Master's sons was before me. It was the definition of being trapped between a rock and a hard place.

But again, that wasn't what I needed to focus on now. So, as I looked at the man before me, I readied myself for battle. But this one would be a battle of wills. One I was determined to win.

CHAPTER NINE

PULLING ON THE GUARD'S ARM, I commanded the rose vines to clear a space around Brand's ankle. Then I used them to bind the two men together. The thorns bent away from the guard and dug deeper into Brand when he tried to shift his ankle away.

"It will only hurt worse if you move," I warned him, not caring if he did so or not.

The vines would ensure that the two men touched, he couldn't stop them bound as he was.

He threw curses and insult that I ignored as I stood and brushed off my hands. There wasn't anything on them that I needed to wipe off, not yet, but it was a nervous gesture. I had never done something like this before, but I *would* do it now. I was trained in how to do it; I just didn't think it would be necessary.

"You really should leave, Adair." I said, mocking the Prince by using his first name.

An odd rumble came from him, and instead of leaving, he stepped even closer to me.

"Maybe," he said, his voice calm despite my rude tone. "But it's my man that you're going to save."

His voice was confident that I would be able to fix this, I only wished I were as sure as he was. My head tilted to the side as I looked at him out of the corner of my eye.

"You filthy bitch, how dare you betray the guild? He raised your worthless life, and this is how you repay him?" Brand said, his voice both angry and desperate.

I hummed, though I didn't agree with him at all. I would have preferred to be a beggar on the streets than have to deal with Jyria's version of *kindness*.

Seeing that his words weren't working when I took a step closer, he went still, staring at me with something I didn't like in his eyes. I knew that look; it was one I had worm myself more than once. It was the look of someone who had accepted their death, and planned to make the person killing them hurt as much as they did before they died.

"I guess so," I agreed, pulling one of my knives and drawing a long line down his chest making sure it wasn't deep enough to kill him.

I didn't want him dead just yet, I only needed him to get as close to it as possible without really killing him. He hissed in a breath, a strange smile coming to his face.

"This is just like old times," he said as I remained silent, drawing another line down his chest with my blade. "I guess turnabout is fair play."

My hand paused, shaking the slightest bit before I ran it once more down his chest again, this time a bit deeper. A slight growl came from the Prince behind me and the three remaining people stepped up to form a semi-circle around us.

The next cut I made was down his arm, the vines drawing back as I made the slow line from shoulder to elbow. He grunted in pain, panting and sweating, but not saying anything.

"This would be much easier for you if you just released him," I told Brand, my voice flat.

"But then I wouldn't get the joy of turning you into a monster just like the rest of us," he croaked.

"I've always been a monster," I told him. "It just wasn't the same kind as the rest of you."

Ignoring the others around me, I drew the knife down his other arm. I was trying to keep my emotions out of this, my horror and disgust with myself growing with every new slice I made. Before, when I had been fighting for my own life, it had been in self-defense. This was different. I was torturing an unarmed and defenseless man.

Sure, he was here to kill me, but at this point in time he was no more capable of it than a child would be.

The next few minutes were silent as I continued to open wounds along his body, his face growing more and more pale as time went on. He was almost there, and I looked down at the guard, wondering how I was supposed to accomplish the next part of my plan.

"What's his name?" I asked the men beside me, gesturing down towards the man at my feet before quickly hiding my blood-soaked hands.

The image was disturbing, and I didn't want to upset them anymore than I already had.

"Why?" The young knight asked, his face both covered with disgusted horror and curiosity.

He was an odd one, but I didn't sense any bad vibes from

him. I wasn't sure why the Prince hadn't said anything about his leaving when the others did, but I could also understand him wanting to stay.

There was a lot in this world that was wrong and dark, and allowing him to get a glimpse of that early on would help if something ever happened while he was out there. It was a way to harden the young man to violence.

Brand chuckled, the sound full of pain.

"Don't tell a monster your name, it will only mean bad things for you," his voice was a dry crackle, but his words weren't a lie.

"Yes, but us monsters have ways of finding things out anyway, I was just trying to save time," I told him, knowing that I would be able to get the information myself long before Brand died.

"His name is Garth," Merrick said, surprising me and the young knight.

"Well, seems like you've managed to gain their trust." Brand said as I made another cut down his chest. "How long will it be before you turn against them? Hmmm? Do you think they're going to let you live after this, knowing that you'll betray them?"

He was trying to make a dig at me, telling me that they were going to kill me, but I already knew that.

"My death was assured as soon as they picked me up yesterday," I told Brand, getting the satisfaction of seeing surprise cross his face. "I knew it, and they knew it. I'm doing this purely for my own pleasure."

It wasn't pleasure I was feeling, but anger and disgust. And despite the pain I knew he was feeling, the man wouldn't stop giving me that stupid, smug smirk of his. Every cut only seeming to make it grow wider, even as I grew to hate myself even more.

The smile on his face seemed to mock me. Like he was telling me that I would never be anything than the monster I was right now. That I was finally showing my true colors.

Letting my emotions get the better of me, I lashed out and dragged the dagger down through one of his eyes. Brand cried out in pain, that smile finally disappearing, and I took a deep breath to get myself back under control.

A warm hand came down on my shoulder, the weight soothing as it allowed me to settle my turbulent emotions.

Brand chuckled, pain in every breath, "Now we really *are* even aren't we?"

"Monsters who match," I agreed.

The Prince's fingers tightened briefly on my shoulder and I wasn't sure what to think about the fact that he was still touching me. Even knowing what I had done. What I was doing even *now*. He wasn't scared to touch me.

"Do I get to see your face again before I die?" Brand asked, and there was something in his voice that made me pause my instinctive response to tell him to screw off.

Thinking over all the reasons he would want to see my face; I could only come up with two. He could have just wanted to see what he had done to me, the only person aside from the Guild Master himself that had ever gotten a hit in. Or, and the more likely scenario, was that he wanted to see me suffer before he died.

Showing my face wasn't something I liked to do. It gave those around me the ability to track me down, but it also made them wary of me. More so than seeing me in a cloak. It was an odd reaction, and one that I hadn't quite figured out, but suspected was a curse from my own people. Even before Brand had gotten to me it had happened.

"I'll make you a deal," I started, seeing some excitement fill his eyes.

"And what's that?" He asked, still in pain, but eager as well.

"I'll let you see my face, but you have to release the guard without harming him," I told him, my voice hard.

I wasn't going to budge on that. I was already dead, and I was fairly sure that three out of the four men around me had already seen my face once before, so it wouldn't be as effective as he was hoping. But on the off chance that they decided to kill me immediately, I needed to ensure that the guard was free.

"How do I know you'll keep your word?" He asked, but when I just silently stared at him, he scoffed a laugh. "Right."

"Your choice," I told him.

When he remained silent, I raised my blade once more. We didn't have time for him to stall.

"Alright!" He snarled, just as my blade was about to touch his skin. "I'll release him, but you have to finish me off while looking me in the eye."

"A deal is struck," I agreed, magic swirling between us as the deal solidified with unbreakable magic.

"Damn," He panted, a smug smile on his face. "I forgot you could do that."

I didn't really do anything, my magic created a contract and put it in place all on its own. It was a part of what I was, and it took more effort to stop it, than to let it happen. The only good part was that both parties had to state their intentions, and the deal was only struck once I said those exact words. Until that point, both parties were free to change their minds.

Brand barely glanced down at the guard before the man gasped and sat up. I immediately removed the vines from his wrist, and bent to drag him away, not wanting to allow Brand anytime to do something to him.

"Your turn, *Kitten*," he sneered, using the nickname the Prince had earlier.

I thought about asking the Prince to turn away, if only so I didn't have to see his reaction to the thing that caused people to become upset upon seeing me, but I wouldn't bother. I knew that he wouldn't agree to do it.

There wasn't a point in wasting time with hesitation, I had agreed to this, and he had held up his end of our bargain. I would weather the fall out like I usually did. Alone. Forcing a calm I didn't feel, I shrugged off the Prince's hand when he touched my shoulder again, not wanting his comfort, and not wanting him to have a hold on me when I killed Brand.

He dropped his hand down to his side, squeezing it into a fist before I started to ignore him.

"I...what's going on?" The guard that was slowly climbing to his feet asked, confusion on his face.

He would have been aware of what had happened while under Brand's control, but it took a moment for those memories to settle back into place.

"You're fine, Garth," I told him, my voice taking on a musical quality as his gaze moved to where my face was under my cloak. "You should go to your quarters to rest. Your body is going to be sore as soon as it figures out that it's free."

Nodding, a blank look similar to the one he wore while under Brand's control covered his face. He turned without saying another word and headed off in the direction of where I was assuming his room was.

Brand snickered, watching the man wander away.

"We really are the same," he finally turned back to me. "It's too bad you were such a Princess. We could have taken the guild by storm. Ruled over all those idiots and taken what we wanted."

"There's no point in ruling a people that would take any chance to kill you that they could," I told him, stepping closer as my hand raised to my hood.

Not bothering to wait, I pulled it from my head, letting him see my face for the first time in years.

His eyes widened and hate flashed across his face before he got control of himself and his gaze came to rest on the scar that he had given me. It started just above my eyebrow and cut through my eye to just above my cheek bone. It had whitened to match the other markings on my face, though it was obviously not the same.

There was a shift behind me, my long hair blowing in the breeze even though it was in a ponytail. The top was in a braid that ran the entire length of my head, the curls making it more voluminous and the color different than any I had ever seen on a human before.

It was a silver color that faded to an off blue, the blue a perfect match for my one eye, and the silver a perfect match to the one that Brand had injured. I could see out of it fine, the injury had healed, but the color of it had never returned to normal. It just made my face that much more unsettling to others.

But what was probably the most damming of all my features, and what my pulled-back hair reveled, was the way my ears came to a point at the tops, giving away what I was.

"It's too bad that you won't live long enough to see all the people you've saved die by the guild's hand," he said with a smile, right as I took his head from his shoulders.

"The guild can't touch them," I said softly to the dead man before   me.

CHAPTER TEN

A SOUND CAME FROM BESIDE ME, and I turned without thinking, meeting the gaze of the young knight, and watching as a hateful gleam glazed over his eyes.

I pulled my hood back up, but it was too late. Raising my arm up, my staff grew to cover my forearm just in time to stop his blade from making contact.

Curses came from beside me as Merrick cast a spell to freeze the young man where he stood.

"What was that about?" Xavier asked, looking between the knight and me.

"Nothing," I muttered, turning to walk back through the garden towards the room I had woken up in.

I left the bodies, not caring who dealt with them now. More men would be coming for me, the Guild Master wasn't going to stop, but I would be either dead, or gone long before then.

"He'll be fine in a few moments," I called back before walking into the castle like I owned it.

My shoulders were back, and I was doing my best to put on an air of confidence. But something in me had broken with the young night's attack, something I did my best to pretend didn't exist.

I was an assassin, a killer that skulked around in the night murdering people. I wasn't supposed to have a heart that was so easily broken by a stranger's actions. So, I pretended that I didn't. I pretended that there wasn't a small part of me that was happy the others came to my defense. Or that that same small part of me was sad that I would be dying by those same men's hands.

None of them had flinched as they watched what I had done, though the young night had been upset, he hadn't shied away like I had myself. I wasn't as strong as I liked to pretend, and running away to hide in a borrowed room was proof of that.

No one followed me, and I appreciated it. I was assuming that they were taking care of their man, and that they had spells in place to stop me from leaving. I wasn't going to test them; I wasn't planning to leave.

The guild was already after me, I couldn't fake my death now, and I had a feeling that the Prince and his men weren't quite done with me yet. I wasn't sure what they wanted, but this was the fourth time they had found me, and I was still alive. That made me think that they wanted something from me and just hadn't gotten around to it.

The same thing as before happened as I moved through the halls; people moved out of my way, sometimes even going as far as to treat me like I was out to get them. I ignored them as best as I could, at least until a young woman stepped directly into my path and stopped.

"Can I help you?" I asked when she didn't move and continued to stare at me with anger, and something else.

I wasn't sure what I had done to her, but this wasn't completely unexpected.

"You need to leave," she said, and I tilted my head as I looked at her.

"No," I said, not bothering to tell her that I was pretty sure that I *couldn't* leave.

Her face flushed, but she didn't move closer to me. Under her anger was also a healthy dose of fear. It created a sour scent in the air, and I was sure she wouldn't like to know that.

"The Prince doesn't need people like you around. You're an ugly, good-for-nothing person, and you need to die. All you'll do it get him hurt, and I'm here to protect him from you." Her voice shook, the sound almost imperceptible if I hadn't still had my senses heightened, I may have missed it.

"He can take care of himself," I said as she made a strange noise and I looked her over.

She was in nicer clothes than a maid would be, and from the way she held herself I thought she was a lady of the higher court. A young woman was peeking from around a doorway further up the hall, but the fear and curiosity lining her face let me know that she wasn't going to join the fight I knew the woman in front of me was trying to start.

But for what reason? I couldn't figure it out. She didn't seem like she wanted to be here exactly, but the anger and fear were genuine.

"Who are you to the Prince?" I asked her, curious as to why she would feel the need to defend him when it was obvious that he could handle himself.

I didn't think she knew him well at all.

"I'm his future wife, if you must know, and I don't like scum like you hanging around him." She said, puffing out her chest.

The words rang false, and I looked at the surprise on the hiding girls face to confirm the fact that it was wishful thinking on the girl's part.

"Oh, really?" I asked, feigning excitement while inside I wanted to laugh. "Congrats, when's the big day?"

"I—it's—we haven't set a date yet," she said, floundering for more information.

"You should really start planning," I told her, smiling to myself. "I've heard weddings are a big deal. Wouldn't want to put off something so important."

"You wouldn't understand," she scoffed, still continuing her lie. "Someone like you will never get married. You'll die soon enough, and then you won't be able to taint the Prince with your nasty presence."

Those words, though they were said without confidence *did* ring true.

"Hm. You're probably right," I agreed, enjoying the slight widening of her eyes. "I wouldn't understand that at all."

The slightest tingle and the deliberate sound of steps came from down the hall. And I had a good idea of who was coming. The way the woman in front of me squared her shoulders like she was about to go to battle let me know that she didn't have a clue that her *fiancé* was approaching us.

"But really," I said as she opened her mouth. "Such an important event should be announced to the world. Should we go and tell the court the good news?"

"What good news?" The Prince's voice said as he came to stand behind me.

The woman in front of me seemed to flush, then pale as she finally realized we weren't alone. Though we never were. This whole situation was odd, and not just because she was confronting me and lying about the reason, but because I had a feeling that she didn't want to be here.

"Why the news of your impending nuptials, of course," I said, making the girl in front of me pale further. "I was just informed of the joyous news."

I couldn't hide all the humor in my voice, though I thought it was hidden pretty well.

"My...wedding..." the Prince repeated, and I felt his eyes burning into the side of my head.

"Yes," I agreed with a nod, smiling under my hood where they couldn't see it. "This young lady..."

I held out my hand to gesture to the woman before me, and she offered her name on instinct.

"Gwendolyn."

"Right, Gwenny here was just telling me all about it." My humor grew as I heard a snicker come from one of the men behind me.

That seemed to snap Gwendolyn out of her fear filled trance and she squared her shoulders.

"She's lying to you, your highness," she said, dropping into a curtsy. "I was simply offering a greeting and she started threatening me to stay away from you. I'm glad you came when you did as I was starting to fear for my life."

Her head was tilted down, but there was a hiccup in her voice that indicated tears. Sure enough, when she tilted her head back up, there were lines of tears running down both her cheeks. She was a great actress.

The girl hiding in the doorway further down looked shocked, and I saw something pass over her face. Terrified, yet determined, she started to step out, but I shook my head subtly. The movement caught her eye, and I did it again when she looked at me. She looked torn, but with a nod, she stepped back into hiding.

It would be much harder for her to escape the witch's clutches than it would be for me. The magic the woman was throwing off was powerful, but she hadn't once tried to reach for it, something else I found odd if she was really trying to threaten me into leaving.

The woman in the alcove's attire, from the brief glimpse of it I had gotten, was that of the castle's maids. She would be forced to stay here, and I knew that the woman in front of me would have much more control of what happened to her than I did.

"Don't lie," she said, seeing my head shake and assuming it was for her. "I'm sorry, my Prince, I tried to be kind, but she was so cruel, and I'm scared that she's going to hurt me."

"What do you have to say about the matter?" The Prince asked, and I knew he was talking to me.

"Nothing, my Prince, nothing at all." My voice was flippant as I stood there, letting the girl spin her web of lies.

The Prince was smart enough to see through them, but I wasn't going to put him in a situation where he had to call her out. Not when I wasn't sure he would. I wouldn't make myself seem like the bad guy any more than I already had. And between the word of a lady of the court and an assassin, I knew who would win. And it was a fight that my skills wouldn't be able to save me from.

There was also the fact that I wasn't sure who this woman was, and I had a feeling that she was important. Even if the Prince didn't like her, he would probably get in trouble for going against her in such an obvious way.

"This sounds serious," he said, though something was off in his tone. "What did she say? How did she threaten you?"

Adair placed a hand on my shoulder, whether it was to keep me still, or for show, I wasn't sure. The look that flashed through Gwendolyn's eyes was much more obvious to figure out. It was a look of pure, unadulterated fear.

"She said all sorts of horrible things that I couldn't bear to repeat," she sniffled, more tears escaping as she let out another sob.

"Oh, I said all sorts of things, alright," I nodded, the Prince's hand feeling heavy on my shoulder. "Like how I thought she was an ugly good for nothing person and that she needed to die."

Gwendolyn's eyes flashed with surprise, then relief before she got it back under control and pulled out more fake sobs. Adair's hand on my shoulder squeezed, not tight enough to cause pain, but enough that I thought it would be more difficult to break the grip. Not that I wouldn't be able to.

"Then she pulled a knife on me," Gwendolyn said, and I stiffened.

It was one thing to threaten someone with words, but if I hadn't already been sentenced to death, her accusation that I had pulled a blade on her would have been a sure-fire way to make sure it happened. She had gone from threats, to attempted murderer in a few minutes time.

"I guess us monsters come in all shapes and sizes," I muttered under my breath.

This had just gotten more complicated, and there wasn't a way that I could see out of this that would end with my life intact and the Prince not in a sticky situation. A strangled chuckle escaped me, but I pretended it was a cough.

"Alright, then I pulled a knife on her," I said finally, the Prince's grip now firm enough it was starting to hurt.

I wasn't sure what he was feeling, but a strangled sound came from behind me, Merrick and Xavier no longer laughing. I had all but sentenced myself to death, but I had given the Prince an easy out. He would be able to deal with the witch in front of me in his own way without repercussions.

More footsteps started to come towards us, and I sighed softly. I just wanted to go and wallow in my borrowed room on my own. What was happening now?

I turned to look behind the Prince, not wanting my back to the new potential threat.

It was funny that the Prince and his friends didn't feel like a threat to me. They never had. It was funny...and concerning.

A few of the guards came into view, the three men familiar. They had been out in the garden earlier, and I watched as they paused when they came upon us. I knew that they had a patrol inside, though this wasn't the usual time that it took place. Maybe the arrival of the other assassins had prompted them to start doing them more often. Or maybe it was the fact that they knew I was here.

Concern was on their face, and I watched as they tried to figure out what was going on. Though when their eyes ran over the tear stained face of the woman in front of me, and then to the Prince's hand on my shoulder, the conclusions that they were coming to were obvious.

That same small part of me broke a little more as I watched, without anyone saying anything, as they condemned me for a crime I hadn't committed.

"What did the blade look like?" Merrick asked, his voice calm even as the guards moved closer with their hands hovering over their weapons.

"What?" Gwendolyn asked as the Prince stepped between me and the guards whose eyes didn't leave me.

Not able to see them anymore, my gaze moved over both Xavier and Merrick, wondering what he was getting at, then turned to face my murderer.

"What did the blade that she pulled on you look like?" Merrick asked again, his tone still calm.

"Like a regular knife," she said, her confusion clear even as my own cleared up. "It was silver, and when she flashed it at me it was terrifying."

"So, the blade she threatened you with was shiny silver?" Xavier asked her again, clarifying what she had said.

"Yes," she agreed, that same fearful look briefly flashing through her eyes as she realized something wasn't right.

"Hey, Adair?" Merrick asked the Prince, "What color was the blade that she used earlier?"

"There were a few, but none of them were regular silver blades," the Prince answered as his hand finally relaxed on my shoulder.

His hand would leave a bruise, but I wasn't going to complain. They had just found a way to clear me of my supposed crime, and I didn't know how to feel about it yet. Confusion over the whole point of clearing my name ran through me. Why would they do it if they were just going to turn around and kill me anyway?

"What?" Gwendolyn said again as she looked between us. "What do you mean she used a blade that wasn't silver? Did she threaten you too, my Prince?"

I snorted. "As if I would be that dumb."

The words escaped before I could filter them, and I heard a deep chuckle come from behind me.

"You could probably take me," the Prince said with humor. "If you actually fought full out."

The thought of that fight was almost exciting. I knew I wouldn't actually want to harm this man, but I would love to go head to head with him. I wasn't completely sure what he was, but I knew he wasn't human.

"That would be fun," I said, once again my words slipping out without my permission.

"Then we'll plan on it sometime soon," he said, surprising me.

"You're going to let her live after she threatened to kill me? You heard what she said, she agreed that she said it," Gwendolyn said, her tears drying up as fear took its place.

"My Prince?" One of the guards stepped forward.

But unlike the rest of them he seemed to see the woman in front of me as the enemy in this situation, and not myself.

"Gwendolyn and her family will be leaving the castle grounds immediately. The lord's request will be denied, and he is to be told the reason for the denial was due to his daughter." Adair said causing me and the girl in front of me to make sounds of surprise.

"Why would you do that My Prince? She threatened me. Why would you reward this thief for pulling a weapon on one of your own people?"

"While I'm sure she's pulled a weapon on many of my people, she didn't threaten you here today. Despite what you both said earlier, I'm sure my personal guard would never do something like that."

"Your *what*?" Me and Gwendolyn said at the same time.

When I turned my head to look up, the Prince had a smile on his face and a gleam in his eye.

"I didn't agree to that," I told him, too confused by his words to think about what he was saying, and what it meant.

"I know," he agreed, still smiling.

"Your Highness?" The other guards questioned.

"Two of you can escort Miss Gwendolyn to gather her belongings and then you can take her and her family to the gates."

"Yessir," two of the men said, leaving the one that had stepped forward earlier here with us as the others stepped up on either side of the woman before me, neither of them meeting my gaze.

"You'll regret this," she said quietly enough I don't think she expected me to hear it.

And while I had no doubt that she had come here with the intention to threaten me into going away, her parting words didn't feel like that at all. It was like she was warning me under the guise of a threat, and my eyes sharped as I looked her over.

With a final huff, she turned on her heel and started to stalk away. When she got to the doorway the young maid was hiding, she paused. Her eyes seemed to take in the huddled young woman and something like understanding lit her gaze.

A look of regret stole over her determined face and I pulled my arm free of the Prince. Magic ran through me as I pulled on my speed just as she raised her arm. I stepped in front of the young woman just in time for Gwendolyn's palm to connect with my face. My head jerking to the side with the force, though it only stung a little through my hood.

A gasp came from behind me, and a growl and cursing came from the men down the hall. Gwendolyn stared at me with fear in her eyes, but I didn't retaliate, just turned to watch her.

"She wasn't the reason you were caught in your lies, and the fact that you tried to retaliate against her for getting yourself in trouble proves how spoiled and immature you are." My words, despite their harshness, were said with understanding.

She shuddered, an odd expression coming to her face as she lifted her hand for another blow, but the Prince's growled words echoed down the hall and stopped her in her tracks.

"That's enough," he slowly stalked closer to us, his moves predatory as his eyes glowed gold. "You are to leave the castle grounds at once, and you and your family are banned from this kingdom until you can apologize for your actions here today."

The guards stepped closer to her, knowing better than to press the Prince right now. My eyes were locked on the Prince's face, his eyes flashing gold once again before returning to their normal green color. I was fascinated by the change, but something in me relaxed at the same time.

Safe.

Merrick and Xavier were also watching the Prince, but they were watching him with concern and not the same calm that I was.

As soon as Gwendolyn was out of sight, I turned to the young woman and tilted my head at her in a nod. Lifting my hand, I placed it on her head as her shoulders relaxed and she closed her eyes. She didn't flinch away from me, but swayed toward me instead.

"I appreciate your help earlier," I told her softly as she opened her eyes to look at me.

"But I didn't do anything," she whispered right back, forgetting that the men were behind me. "She was trying to get you killed, and I just stood back and watched."

Tilting my head, I watched her for a moment before I bent forward and placed a kiss against her forehead, a promise and a spell of protection. An outline of my lips glowed for a moment as I pulled away before seeping below her skin. Merrick gasped, and the young woman's eyes flashed to him as she remembered he was there, her cheeks going pink.

"Sometimes just being willing to step up is enough." I told her, pulling her attention back to me. "Thank you."

And I meant it. She was the only person who had ever been willing to put their own safety on the line for me. I wouldn't forget it anytime soon.

CHAPTER ELEVEN

THE GUARD SLOWLY WALKED DOWN the hall, leaving us alone as the three men behind me seemed to almost shift closer. The young woman nodded but didn't look like she believed me as I continued to look at her.

Taking a step back, I turned and continued on my way, all my turbulent emotions from earlier having settled.

"You just..." Merrick's voice trailed off as he followed behind me, the awe and confusion clear.

"Yes," I agreed, knowing what he was getting at.

"But I didn't think your people still did that?" He questioned, something odd in his voice. "I thought that ability was going extinct."

I paused in my steps, turning to face him outside the door to the room I had been staying in.

"They are not *my* people, not anymore." I told him, the anger in my voice enough to make him back up a step. "And I can do many things that were supposed to be lost to us long ago. You would do well to remember that. After all, they are partly *your* people as well, aren't they?"

I was calling him out and I saw his face pale just a bit as he looked at the Prince. It wasn't like he was scared the Prince hadn't known, more like he was worried about something else altogether.

"How did you know?" It was Xavier who asked, confirming that it was something else that had worried the other man.

His friends already knew what he was.

"That doesn't matter," I said, turning and opening the door.

There was a split-second warning as the spell went off, but I still just managed to slam the door shut in time, trapping me alone in the room as the bomb went off.

I woke to find a golden eyed man leaning over me, concern and fear in his face as a colorful orb glowed around us.

"She's coming to," the Prince growled, his voice deeper than normal.

"Good," Xavier said, and I realized that he was leaned over my legs, pulling on something that made me wince.

Another growl came from the Prince and my eyes flew back up to see the shadow of shimmering scales fade back under his skin. The longer I met his gaze, the more the gold in his eyes faded, though it would flash when I winced with pain. Aside from the oddness of it all, it confirmed that my hood really was off, and I wasn't imagining the lack of its comforting weight.

"You're not trying to kill me?" My words came out as a question, even though I had meant it to be a statement.

"No," Merrick answered, the Prince still just staring at my face. "But someone else is."

My eyes flicked toward the man speaking as he finally lowered the shielding spell.

I pushed myself to sitting, though the Prince placed a hand on my back to help me stay up. I watched as Xavier used his fingers and a blade to dig more shrapnel from my legs.

"Yes, but not all of those that want me dead actually know *how* to do it."

It wasn't the fire the bomb released that had caused me to go down, but sharp arrowheads and other objects that had come flying out of it. The objects made of stone weren't what had done much damage, but the actual bits of iron that had been used.

I wasn't allergic to iron like most of my people, but it wasn't something I had an affinity for either, so I wasn't able to stop it from causing damage when it was used against me. Like any other weapon, it would hurt me if they were able to make a hit.

Xavier's hand was shaking as he tried to dig out more of the smaller items, and I reached out my own hand to lay it on his.

"Thank you, but I can get the rest. You guys should make sure the area is secure. While I can agree that it looked like this was meant for me, there is still a price on both the Prince's and *your* head."

He looked up at me like he wasn't sure what to do. I brought out one of my own knives, the blue color beautiful as it glimmered in the fading light that came from the hole that had been blown in the castle wall.

Not waiting for him to speak, I used my blade to start digging out the remaining pieces, not being nearly as careful as Xavier had been. The Prince growled when I dug too deep, but I ignored his snarling curses and kept going until, with the help of Xavier, we got the rest of them out. Despite my words, I *had* needed his help to get a few of the ones in my arms and sides.

Overall, the damage was minimal. I wondered if the person who had set this trap had known that they wouldn't be able to cause much damage, or if they had miscalculated.

I accepted the Prince's help to reach my feet, but didn't keep hold once I was standing. There were other guards and castle personnel running around, but they were keeping their distance from the four of us. I couldn't help but wonder if that was because they were worried about the Prince, or if they were scared to come closer.

A few of them were sneaking peeks at us, but none of them were showing the usual aggression I was used to when they looked at my face. I saw concern, fear, and more than one person who showed pity and curiosity when they saw the scar through my eye. But none of the hatred and anger.

Still, I pulled the hood of my cloak up so that my face was once again hidden.

"What did you do?" I asked, not directing my question to any one of them, but hoping they would answer.

There was no way the people weren't freaking out about seeing my face without something intervening.

"After the first time the Prince ordered them away, we didn't do anything." Xavier said as he wiped his forehead and stepped closer to us.

I wasn't sure I believed him, but I didn't see what he would gain from lying. That didn't mean I was going to start walking around without my hood, however. My identity was out, and there was no chance of me being able to disappear, but the habit was too deeply ingrained inside me at this point.

"Why did you shut the door?" The Prince asked me, speaking for the first time since he had announced that I was waking up.

"What?" I asked, not sure what he was getting at.

"You felt the spell going off, I saw it on your face, but you stepped in and shut the door, not out. I would have been able to handle that blast much better than you; you should have stepped behind me, not in front." The longer he spoke the more upset he seemed to become.

"It was instinct," I told him, confused about what was happening.

I wasn't going to use him as a shield, that wasn't right. But it *had* been instinct. I hadn't thought for a moment to use any of them as a shield. Though, the Prince was right, he probably wouldn't have been injured by the magical bomb at all.

Something else that concerned me, but that I would have to figure out later, was that the Prince had just confirmed that he could see my face from under my cloak. He really had been able to see me this entire time.

"We'll have to work on that," he said, breaking me out of my troubled thoughts, and the others nodded in agreement.

"I—what?"

Nothing that he was saying was making sense.

How did everything get so messed up? Wasn't he supposed to be the one killing me? What was he doing telling people that I was his guard? And now he was telling me to save myself and use him as a shield? I didn't understand him at all.

"We're a team, that means we work together as a team." Merrick said, coming closer. "In this instance the Prince was the best able to handle the blast, so we would have let him handle it. If it was something else, we would have figure it out."

"What does that have to do with me?" I asked him, still not

sure why they were telling me all this.

Sure, I knew what they were saying, understood what they were suggesting, but I didn't know *why*.

"What does that have to do with me? I'm an assassin that was sent here to kill both the knight and the Prince. You should be holding me in a cell while you figure out the best way to get rid of me. You *shouldn't* be telling me how I messed up and should have used the Prince as a shield to save myself a little pain." My voice was growing more exasperated, and that feeling only continued to grow when they didn't say anything, and just smiled at me.

"Your Highness, we didn't find anything else of concern, though Miss Gwendolyn and her father have both disappeared like you had guessed." The same young guard from earlier said as he stepped over some of the debris.

Another evil presence appeared on my radar, and I sighed. Turning towards the three men surrounding me again, I dropped my head against the nearest man's chest. I was too tired for this.

Merrick made a sound of surprise, and I smiled. Slowly, his arms came up around me, one on the back of my head, the other between my shoulder blades. It was a surprisingly nice feeling.

"We should duck," I mumbled into his chest.

"What?" He asked.

I lifted my head, knowing I wouldn't be able to move fast enough, but that they would.

"Duck."

None of the men around me missed a beat, but I was surprised when Merrick brought me with him as he hit the floor. I grunted, but all of the arrows that were aimed at us either missed or hit the magical shield Merrick put up.

"He's all yours," I told the men staring at me. "He can produce arrows like me, but he isn't as fast. He can shoot up to ten at a time, though."

The Prince looked at Xavier, who smiled an unkind smile.

"Got it."

Then the knight stood and ran at the hole in the wall, heading directly for the area that the arrows had come from.

Instead of standing with the Prince and Merrick, I just burrowed farther into the floor, spreading the bits and pieces of debris, and making myself a nice nest of broken stone and wood. My body was done. Between all the assignments and injuries I had sustained, I was too tired to stand again. While I knew I had slept a bit this morning, it had been magically induced, and not actual rest.

"Kitten?" Adair said as he bent over me exchanging a look of concern with Merrick.

"Ionia," I muttered, accidently correcting him.

His face changed to one of surprise, but I was too tired to curse myself and regret my impulsive decision to tell him my real name.

"I like Kitten better," he said softly as my eyes started to close.

"Me too," I agreed.

Then I passed out, too tired to even keep my eyes open.

"You're going to give the Prince a heart attack if you keep doing things like that," Merrick muttered as consciousness found me again.

I was feeling immensely better, and I knew this time that it was Merrick who had helped me heal so fast.

"Why?" I asked as I sat up in an unfamiliar bed.

This room was much bigger than the one that I had been placed in before, and so was the size of the bed. I knew this room, this bed.

"Why am I in the Prince's bed?" I asked, looking over at the tired looking advisor. "You should really get some sleep."

He chuckled at my words, standing from the chair that he had been sitting in.

"Good idea," he agreed, coming and flopping onto the bed beside me.

I stared at him, not sure what I had expected, but this wasn't it. There was less than a foot of space between us, but soon enough he was breathing softly, fast asleep.

"I'm starting to think you guys have a death wish," I said softly, looking up at Adair as he came into the room.

His eyes went from his friend asleep beside me to where I was sitting in his bed.

"No, we just trust you." He said, keeping his voice just as soft as mine had been.

"That's the exact same thing," I told him.

He smiled at me, something about him more relaxed that it had been since I had met him.

Something had changed, and I wasn't sure what it was. Not understanding what was happening was starting to become a common thing, and I didn't like it.

"You're one of us now, as unconventional as that may be.

We've all agreed that there's something about you that we would like to keep around. And you've saved all of our lives more than once, knowingly or not."

I opened my mouth, but he smiled and started to talk before I could protest.

"I know you don't have anywhere else to go, and honestly, I think you're the perfect person to have on our side."

"But I was sent to kill you," I argued. "I kill people for a *living*."

He nodded his head in agreement. "You did, but we did our research after you were able to make it into my room that night."

He walked closer, taking the chair that Merrick had been sitting in a few minutes before.

"We know all about those that you've killed, and we also know about the people you've saved." He gave me an odd look, like he wasn't sure what to make of me, and I was just as confused by him. "What I don't understand, is how someone like you could have been trained and raised in the guild."

"And what kind of person do you think I am, exactly?"

"The   kind   with   a   heart."

CHAPTER TWELVE

I STARED AT HIM FOR A MOMENT where he was sitting in the chair. There was a smile on his face, and he didn't seem to doubt his words one bit as they left his mouth. Though, knowing who I was, and what I had done, I didn't see how that was possible.

"You're wrong, Prince," I told him, slowly moving towards the end of the bed so that I wouldn't wake Merrick. "I've just chosen to go against the Guild Master. It had nothing to do with having a heart."

He hummed, but he didn't seem to believe me.

"Where are you going?" He asked me as I stood up.

"To wash up," I told him heading towards his bathroom.

I probably should have asked him if I could use it, but I felt dirty, and I *needed* to get clean.

"If you want, you can leave your clothes outside the door, I'll have Maribelle wash them for you." He said softly.

I looked at the Prince, not sure I could trust that I would get them back.

He moved over to sit in a chair, looking calm as he watched me.

"She's the one from the hallway that you helped earlier," he said, like that would make me more inclined to trust them with my belongings.

And, strangely, it did. There was something pure about Maribelle, something that let me know that I could trust her. Tilting my head to the side, I looked the Prince over. He was able to read me easily even when he couldn't see my face before, and I didn't like it.

"And what about my weapons? Where do you suggest I put them while my things are being washed? And what would I wear while I wait for them to dry?"

His smile widened and he stood, moving over to his chest of drawers. Pulling open the top drawer he pulled out a shirt and a pair of pants with a waist that tightened.

"You can wear my things while we wait, and as for your weapons," he moved over and pulled a long thin case out from under the bed. "You can place them in here."

I moved closer to where he was opening the case on the bed, curious about it. The magic coming from it was powerful, and though I didn't know exactly what it was, I had a feeling the Prince was offering to let me use something that was very personal to him.

My gaze moved from the long, velvet lined case to the Prince's face. His expression was open and honest, prompting me to trust him. It wouldn't be the biggest deal in the world if he were to take them, I would just make more. But it took time, pain, and magic to make them, and I was worried I wouldn't have enough time before the next attack to do it.

I started pulling all the weapons from my person, my blades gleaming like the jewels they were made from. Ruby, sapphire, citrine, and so on. My enchanted sticks were next. Sticks was the wrong word, but they looked like branches with swirling filigree imbedded inside them. Jewels were also placed along them, the weapons beautiful and designed to grow and morph into what I needed them to be at the time. I called them wands, similar to the objects that some witches used to direct their magic. Only I used mine to hold it.

The Prince watched me, the gleam in his eyes letting me know that he appreciated my weapons. But with the way he watched them, I wasn't worried he would steal them from me. There was nothing nefarious about him in this moment that would cause me to worry.

His hand reached out like he would caress one of the wands. The one that would morph into my bow when I infused it with my magic, but he didn't quite touch it.

Eying him for a moment, I reached out and grabbed it, placing it in his hands so that he could get a closer look. His gaze met mine, letting me know that he understood how heavy this show of trust was. It wasn't only that I was trusting him to hold and not break it, but that his energy and intentions weren't bad. It was also a way of me telling him that I didn't think he meant me any ill will.

If he intended me harm in any way shape or form my weapons would lash out at him on their own. It was part of the reason that fae weapons were so coveted. Every single one of them, once bonded to the user, would never allow someone else to brandish them unless that user trusted the person implicitly. That, and they weren't easy to use if you weren't fae-born yourself. Nearly impossible, truth be told.

While I wasn't there yet, I did trust this Prince not to cause me harm right now, and my weapons could sense that.

"They're beautiful," he whispered reverently, running his finger over the markings. "Who made them?"

I looked at him for a moment before picking up a pair of short darker sticks and allowing them to grow into a pair of short swords, the same ones I had used to take Sar's head earlier.

"I did."

His head jerked over to me at my words, and his eyes were wide with surprise. A whole new appreciation for the weapons entered his eyes, and he started to look over the one I had handed him more closely. I leaned closer and ran my hand above the weapon, watching as one of the sigils unwound and spread between the ends of the branch as it grew and stretched until it formed a bow.

The weapon looked a bit small in the Prince's hands, but it was made for me, so that wasn't a surprise.

"Your work is beautiful," he said honestly, looking at me with that same appreciation on his face.

"Thank you," I told him with a bit of a blush, allowing both weapons to go back to their original forms and placing my wands in the case.

He followed my lead and placed my bow back in the case, making sure to be gentle. It made me smile to see him being so careful. While I was being gentle myself, they weren't delicate in the least. My staff took the full brunt of Sar's axe without getting a scratch, but it was nice that he was being so considerate.

"You'd think he was touching your underthings," Merrick said in a groggy voice as he sat up.

I chuckled as Adair put on an exasperated face.

"In a way, he was," I said jokingly, the Prince's gaze heating as he looked at me, some of the gold poking through.

"You should make us weapons like that. We would be the envy of all the guards," the advisor said, still sounding half asleep.

"Oh, I should, huh?" I asked him, amused.

"We're a team, so we should all have beautiful weapons made by a beautiful woman," his voice was matter of fact, but he fell back to the bed and was asleep again as soon as they were out of his mouth.

The Prince was laughing, but I was in shock. He thought I was beautiful?

"Leave it to him to be the first one to try and charm you," Adair said with a shake of his head. "And while he was still half-asleep, no less."

"The first?" I asked, not really listening to what I was saying, still hung up on what Merrick had muttered.

"Go shower. Your weapons will be here when you get out," the Prince said, shutting the case and leaving it on the bed.

A spell snapped into place as soon as it was closed, but the expected anxiety at having my weapons out of reach never came. So, I nodded and pulled my cloak off, setting it on top of the case as a promise that I would be back for them.

The Prince's eyes roved over my form, his gaze taking in my skintight armored outfit with the same gleam of appreciation as before. Thought this time there was a different sort of heat in his eyes.

"Did you make that as well?" He gestured to my clothing, the same sigils and filigree running throughout it as the ones on my weapons.

"Yes," I agreed with a nod.

My cloak had the same markings, if you were to look close enough, all of the items made by me using natural fae made materials and magic. It had taken me some time to get it right, but it was tougher than any other armor around, and had the added benefit of being imbibed with magic. That meant magical attacks had less of an impact. Most of them, at least.

"You're very skilled," Adair said. "And I would pay you handsomely if you would consider Merrick's words. We would love to have even a single weapon crafted by you."

I tilted my head at him, my hair falling over my shoulder as I did so without the magic in my cloak to keep it back. I considered what he said, not about the money, that wasn't really a concern of mine, but about making weapons for them.

"I'll consider it. But know that if I ever decide to create them, you would need to be involved." I told him, and curiosity lit up his gaze. "You wouldn't be able to wield them against me, either."

"We wouldn't even if we could."

I doubted that, but I let it go.

"I'll think about it," I told him, and he nodded.

"That's all I can ask."

With a nod in return, I turned and headed into the bathroom for my shower, taking the Prince's clothes with me.

I stood in the bathroom, freshly showered, and dressed in the Prince's clothes...and I felt like a child. His clothing was *huge* on me.

"You alright in there, Kitten?" Adair called through the door.

"Yes," I said, taking a deep breath before I opened the door and walked out into his bedroom.

A smile lit up the Prince's face, and I could tell that he was holding back a chuckle.

"Don't you dare laugh," I warned him, holding up a finger in warning.

He snickered, my intimidation tactic failing while I was drowning in fabric.

Xavier walked into the room, and when he saw me he did a double take.

"Ionia," he said, the sound of my name shocking me as he looked like he was torn between laughter and concern. "Where are your clothes?"

"They're being washed," The Prince said, still laughing at my expense.

I frowned at him, but there wasn't anything I could do at the moment.

"Aww, don't pout," Xavier said, coming to put his arm around my neck. "You'll get your clothes back soon enough."

"I'm not pouting," I said with a glare, pushing at the arm around my neck.

It hit me, and not for the first time, how comfortable I was around these men. How the fact that I had never willing let someone else touch me before them never even entered my mind. It just felt so natural around them, like I had been doing it all my life.

I knew what the Prince meant by what he had said earlier, and I could kind of agree. Though I was wary of the feelings I had around them. It wasn't normal to bond to someone so quickly. But did that make it wrong? Was it a bad thing to be so comfortable with these guys so soon? I didn't think it was.

Weird? Definitely. But I had a hard time believing something that felt this natural would be wrong. Especially when no one was getting hurt.

"Well, I've come with news," Xavier said as he launched himself onto the bed, waking Merrick as he did so. "They found Gwendolyn and her father, and she's claiming that they were under a spell and she shouldn't be held responsible for her actions."

"No, she wasn't," I disagreed before realizing that it wasn't my place to say anything.

Though, I knew something wasn't right. I wasn't sure that she had totally been here of her own free will, but I didn't think it was magic that had caused her actions.

"I agree with Ionia, there were no spells on her while she was with us in the hall," Merrick said, rubbing his eyes as he sat up. "Did she admit to having something to do with the attack?"

I looked at them surprised. I shouldn't have been, it made perfect sense that she had been part of the attack, but I honestly hadn't put two and two together. And I should have.

"She didn't admit it out loud, but it was pretty obvious that she had done something, we just aren't sure what."

My hand rose to touch my cheek, the reminder of her slap flashing through my head.

"She marked me," I said, mostly to myself.

"When she slapped you?" The Prince growled out.

I nodded, looking at him unsure. "It would make sense. I couldn't quite figure out what had caused the spell on the door to the room I was using to trigger. It had felt directed, not random, but I didn't know how someone had been able to target it toward me without something of mine to use."

"No, that makes sense," Merrick agreed. "Maribelle had been

in there a few minutes before to change the sheets, and the fact that she had run into you guys in the halls after that means the spell had already been set. If it had been set for just anyone, Maribelle would have set it off before we even made it to the room."

That was a worrisome thought. I didn't like the idea that my being here had put someone as pure as Maribelle in danger. While I knew Adair and these guys could take care of themselves, the same couldn't be said about the others in the castle.

The guards were trained, well trained, but some of them were human, and that meant that they would have trouble against anyone with magic. It wasn't fair, but it was the truth.

"You're troubled," Adair said, looking at me.

"I think I need to leave," I told him, not expecting the rumble that escaped from his chest and the gold flaring in his eyes, though I continued. "It isn't safe for the others if I stay here."

He shut his eyes and the rumbling stopped.

"I don't think that's a good idea," Merrick said, looking at the Prince out of the corner of his eye. "We can monitor the situation from here and take measures to keep everyone safe. There's no guarantee that if you left they would stop coming. You said yourself that there was a price on both Adair and Xavier's heads."

"That's true," I agreed, feeling my will start to crumble under his use of logic.

"Not only that, but we need to know what were up against, and we need you for that." Xavier said, sparking my memory.

"No, you don't," I said, turning to the door intending to go back to the room I had been staying in.

My magic should have protected the pages I had written from

the blast.

"Where are you going?" Adair asked, following me as Xavier and Merrick both stood from the bed.

"To get something from the room you guys had me sleep in before," I said as I walked into the Prince's common room.

Then I paused, knowing there was something I was forgetting, but not sure what.

"Wait!" I called, turning as all three men looked around for a threat before their gazes fell to me. "Sorry, but where is my cloak?"

"Maribelle is still washing your things," the Prince reminded me.

"I know that, but I need it to go out," I said. "I can't leave this room without it.

I would find something in the Prince's closet to use until my clothing was back.

"No, you don't," Xavier said, but I wasn't listening.

I walked back into the Prince's room and, without asking, walked into his closet. The room was almost as large as his bedroom, and I wondered briefly how someone was expected to wear so many clothes, though I guess that could be because I only owned one real set at this point.

Making my way through the wardrobe, I searched for something that would work in my own cloak's place. Because the garment wouldn't be enchanted, I would need to take care in what I chose.

Seeing a hooded cloak tucked into the back corner, I walked over and grabbed it. I knew even before pulling it over my shoulders that it was going to be too big, but I hadn't realized just how large until almost a foot of fabric pooled around my feet, and the hood, once over my head, came down to my chin.

"Find what you were looking for?" The Prince said as all the men gathered in the doorway chuckled at me.

"Yes," I said, feeling silly in the barrowed clothing and cloak, and wanting to prove that I was fine at the same time.

"Good," he continued to chuckle. "Then let's go."

I nodded, the hood flopping and making the action look even sillier. I couldn't see through this one, but after the way I had barged into his closet and put it on I didn't want to admit that it was giving me issues.

"Right," I grumbled, peering at the floor below my feet and relying heavily on my other senses to get around. "Let's go."

Pushing into his room, I led them all into the hall, making my way to the room I had already woken up in twice. The room that was now nothing more than a pile of rubble.

CHAPTER THIRTEEN

I WAS ALMOST HAPPY THAT I COULDN'T see the faces of the people that we passed on the way. From the feelings I was getting as their eyes burned into me, I would guess that they weren't pleasant. That, or they just found it odd that I was in the Prince's clothes.

"It would seem that you've managed to earn yourself some admirers," Xavier said.

"Uh huh," I agreed, not believing him, but unwilling to pull the hood up to see what he was seeing.

"Can you even see in that thing?" Merrick asked, the humor in his voice obvious.

"Not at all," I said, still refusing to pull the hood back as we continued.

All three of them chuckled, and a small smile escaped me.

It felt like it took forever, even when I knew it didn't really take that long for us to arrive, and I heard movement coming from inside where they were trying to clean up. Magic and money would be used to get the castle itself fixed, and with how loved the royal family was I didn't anticipate that it would take long at all.

And with the Guild Master sending more assassins out, that was a very good thing.

"Will you take your hood off now?" Xavier asked as I carefully picked my way through the rubble.

The hood being in my face was extremely frustrating, but I wasn't sure it would be worth it at this point. There was a good chance that the others around me would react badly to seeing my face, and it wasn't something I wanted to deal with at the moment.

It wasn't just because of what I was, but the curse my own people had placed on me before they tossed me out. It was meant to be a punishment for not living up to their expectations. They hadn't wanted to kill me, I had held a high enough position in the courts that that wasn't really a possibility, but they wanted to ensure that I wasn't able to have an easy life either.

"You don't need it right now," Adair said, standing close enough that I could feel his heat at my side.

"Maybe not, but I'm not going to take it off just to please you, *Your Majesty*." I said sarcastically.

It had nothing to do with him, and I knew he was just trying to be reassuring. But after a lifetime of being ridiculed for being different I found it hard to believe his words. That didn't mean I should be rude to him though; I knew he was only trying to help in his own way.

"Well then, by all means, lead the way," I saw his arm raise to gesture me forward, and to my relief there was no anger in his words as he spoke.

"Right," I agreed, my voice softer this time.

I continued to pick my way through the room, tripping more than once over the cloak and debris. Merrick had stepped forward to help me once, and I allowed him to assist me as my cheeks burned with embarrassment. It was another moment I was grateful for the cloak that I was wearing.

Making my way towards where I knew the desk used to be, I bent over to start digging through the rubble that still remained. The people clearing out the room had made progress in getting it clean, but there was still quite a bit left that needed to be done.

"What are we looking for, exactly?" Merrick asked from nearby, and I heard other people shuffling through the wreckage as well.

"It will be a pile of parchment, blank to all but you three, I would assume," I said softly, distractedly.

"Why only us three?" Adair asked, the sound of large stones rubbing together coming from behind me.

"Unless you trust anyone else that has been in here implicitly, it will only be readable to you guys."

"Interesting," Merrick said, and there was something in his voice that almost made me curious enough to lift my hood and look at him.

"What does that mean?" I asked, turning towards where I knew he was working.

"Does that mean that you trust us?" Xavier asked, his footsteps getting closer to me.

"Does an assassin ever trust anyone?" I asked him in return, not giving him an answer.

Because the truth was...I didn't know.

I felt a connection to them that I didn't understand, and I

knew that they were good people. I had seen enough to know that I didn't think they would intentionally cause me harm, but that didn't mean that it couldn't happen. There was also the fact that I was considered a criminal, and the Prince was the highest power aside from the King that would decide when and how I would pay for the crimes I had committed. Death was almost certain, and though it hadn't been said, I was waiting for the guards to take me into custody at any moment.

The Prince had spouted off about me becoming his personal guard, but I figured that had just been a way to get out of that situation without causing more problems. He had said those words for show and didn't really mean them.

At the same time, he had allowed me to sleep in his bed and wear his clothes. Merrick had said that he trusted me, then he had proven that fact by falling asleep in front of me, *knowing* that I was armed.

Ever since I had met them it felt like my life had been turned upside down. That nothing was as it seemed, and I didn't know how to deal with it. I was also aware that their kindness had easily broken through my defenses and I was growing attached to them. It would be hard to leave them, but I had a feeling that something was coming, and that the day I was forced away could be closer than I wanted it to be.

As I was digging through another pile, I felt a sting as I slid my hand back, and I quickly pulled it out of the small space to see a droplet of blood bead up on the surface of my finger. Sighing, I went to wipe the finger on the cloak before remembering that it wasn't my own and thinking better of it.

Deciding to ignore it, I just dug for the piece of paper that had given me the small cut in the first place, being careful not to get blood on the stack of papers.

For being such a small cut, it was bleeding an awful lot, and I glared at my own finger when it left a smudge on the rocks around me. And despite my best effort, a bit even got on papers as I carefully pulled them out from under another, larger stone.

"Why are you bleeding?" The Prince asked from right behind me, his voice intense.

"Because it sounded like fun," I said sarcastically.

He grunted, and when I looked at him over my shoulder it was to find that his face was right there, eye glowing gold. His face was close enough that one wrong move would cause our noses to touch. The moment was both oddly intimate and disturbing. I wasn't sure what to think, so I didn't, and I raised my hand and pressed it palm first against his face, pushing him away from me.

The move was familiar and instinctual, but I immediately felt awkward. When I pulled my hand away it was to find the Prince looking like he was both unsure of what had just happened, and seconds away from laughing.

"I..." My voice trailed off, unsure what I could say that would explain my actions.

Pain ran through me at the memories I associated with those particular actions, and I had to take a moment to force them out. To forget them, and the person they had reminded me of.

I couldn't come up with anything to explain away what I had done. So, instead, I lifted the bundle of parchment and pressed it against his chest. The heavy bundle made a thump sound as it hit him and caused a few of the people walking past to look at us. The looks they sent me were confused, but I could see the dislike cross their face when they saw what I had done. Not that it hurt the Prince at all. He was too muscular, and if I was right, not at all human. Paper wasn't going to hurt him.

"Here." I said, pulling my barrowed hood back down to cover my face.

He chuckled and sent me a smile as he grabbed the papers from me, gold running briefly through his eyes when he saw the small amount of my blood staining the pages. His eyes looked at my finger, but I wasn't too concerned about the small cut that was finally starting to clot. It wouldn't be an issue for much longer, it was just going to be an annoyance until then.

"Thanks," he said deadpan, finally looking down at the actual papers that I had just handed him.

The ones that would ensure I died at the hands of the guild.

"No problem," I said, standing as his eyes got wider.

His gazed flicked up to meet my own from under my hood, understanding and something unsure there in his eyes. I could understand the look, to an extent, but I didn't want to sit here and talk to him about it.

"I'm going to see how my clothes are coming along," I told him, not answering his unasked questions. "You should probably figure out what your next moves are going to be. And I need to leave before more of the guild members are sent my way."

"I thought we agreed that it was going to be safest for you to stay here," Xavier said, stepping closer to us.

"Things change," I told him, not turning to look at him.

"But..." Xavier started.

"She isn't a prisoner here; she can do what she feels she needs to," Merrick said, and though the words hurt to hear, his tone was soft, and I knew he was saying them for my benefit.

Instead of feeling hurt that he didn't seem to want me here, I needed to think about the best way to keep them all safe. I hadn't been here too long; the Guild Master shouldn't have been able to send that many people. There was still a chance that I would be able to get a head start and set traps that would bring down the number of people after me.

Adair and Xavier still had a price on their head, but I had a feeling I was going to be the first priority for the moment. While he wouldn't have confirmation that I had given the Prince information, he would be able to assume as much.

He was utterly confident that his tactics would stop people from talking, but I wasn't scared of him. There wasn't much he could do to me that he hadn't already done, and my own people had caused me enough pain to last me a lifetime. There was nothing stopping me from betraying him, and sooner or later he would realize that. If he hadn't already.

"Why would you do this?" The Prince asked me, finally standing and forcing me to try and look up at him from under the hood that came down to my chin.

With a growl, I pulled it back far enough that I could meet his eyes. His gaze moved over my face, and it left a trail of heat that made my cheeks want to burn. Bringing with it the urge to pull my hood right back down.

"Why shouldn't I?" I asked him, not answering his question.

His lips compressed into a line, and I could tell that despite the fact he was trying to hide it, he was worried.

"Don't worry, Prince," I said, my voice taking on a sarcastic tone, hiding my real feelings. "I can take care of myself."

"But this—"

"Will be extremely helpful." I interrupted him, my eyes flicking towards the hall and the people that were watching us.

While I was probably being paranoid, I didn't want anyone to know what I had just given him. I hadn't felt anything ill-intentioned from those around us, but people still liked to gossip, and I didn't want this to get to the wrong ears too soon.

"Ionia," he said, the sound of my name on his lips sending

my thoughts scattering.

Only one person had ever said it with that same, longsuffering tone. The image of a male face, hair and eyes almost a direct match for mine, came to mind. Sorrow tried to take my breath, but I shut my eyes, and forced a deep breath to enter my lungs.

He wasn't here, and he was safe.

"Yes, Adair?" I said, my voice hard and quiet.

It wasn't his fault that he had triggered my memories and emotions. He couldn't have known, and it wasn't fair of me to be so rude.

"Sorry," I muttered into the stretching silence.

"This information will be invaluable, but I know the cost of you giving it to me," his tone was softer now, and I bit the inside of my cheek, knowing that I didn't deserve his kindness. "So, why are you handing it over?"

"I'm a known assassin that snuck into this castle with the intention of killing both you and your friend," I countered my hood falling completely off as I looked up at him again. "So, why not execute me?"

There was a gasp from the hallway, but I didn't know if it was because of my words or my face being visible. I tensed, just in case, waiting for an attack that never came. The Prince looked over my face with an unreadable expression. And, unable to meet his gaze, I turned to see two guards staring at me from the destroyed doorway.

The expected hatred flashed over their expressions, but it passed quickly and was instead replaced with something I wasn't familiar with. I shifted, uncomfortable and not at all sure how to deal with someone that didn't try to kill me at first glance.

A growl sounded out from beside me, and the two men glanced at the Prince, turning on their heel and walking away at whatever expression was on his face.

"We all know that you were never going to kill him," Merrick said. "Or Xavier, for that matter. You would have easily been able to do it before we could have responded."

My brow furrowed as I turned to look at him. He was watching me with a humored expression on his face. While I had gotten the drop on them, we all knew that they were powerful men. While I would have been able to get a good shot, it wasn't likely that I would have succeeded and kept my own life.

"We both know that's unlikely," I finally said.

A snort came from the knight just behind Merrick, and my gaze flashed over to him.

"We were far too busy being enamored with you to fight back. You had the advantage, but you didn't take it, and I agree that you were never intending to harm us at all."

"You're wrong," I said, troubled.

Almost without thinking, I pulled my borrowed hood back up and over my face, blocking myself from seeing them. And stopping them from seeing the play of emotions that were starting to overwhelm me.

Sure, what he was saying was true. But I had never been called out for *not* killing someone before. What was wrong with me that I was troubled that they knew that I hadn't been here to kill them? I should have been glad, but I wasn't, and I didn't know why.

"Regardless, I've overstayed my welcome," I said, turning towards the door, and using my other senses to help me navigate through the room without being able to see more than the floor a few feet in front of me. "I'm going to get my clothing and leave as soon as I can."

"We'll see you again soon," the Prince said, his voice utterly confident as he slowly started to follow me out.

The urge to run swept over me, and the feeling of being in a predator's gaze suddenly had me feeling like prey. It wasn't threatening, but I still wanted to run, and I wasn't sure why my body was sending me mixed signals. How could being prey *not* be dangerous?

"Uh huh," I said, not meaning it.

There was no way I was going to come back with the guild after me. Yes, the men behind me were extremely powerful, but that didn't mean that I would use them to make my life easier. The only reason they had met me in the first place was because someone had decided to try and put a price on their heads.

They could handle themselves, and I knew that they would be able to take the assassins that would be sent after them when I was gone. The Guild Master would focus on me until he knew what I had told them, or I was dead. He would try to make sure that his secrets weren't exposed, and I knew that would make me his first priority.

I paused in the ruined doorway, feeling the Prince's heat against my back as he moved to stand behind me.

"Remember that you have a price on your head, Prince." I said, my version of goodbye.

Something inside me wanted to stay, but that was a stupid and useless wish. I couldn't stay, not if I wanted them to live.

Xavier let out a snort, but Adair placed a warm hand on my shoulder, squeezing gently.

"You've made yourself a target, so until we meet again, stay alive." The Prince's words made a lump rise in my throat, but I wasn't going to think too hard about why.

Instead of answering, I walked away. The Prince's hand fell away from my shoulder, and I knew that this was probably the last time I would see them. They were the first people that had seen my face and hadn't reacted with anger and disgust, the first people in general that had treated me as an equal, and not a tool.

That, above anything else, was the reason I was leaving. I had gotten too close, become too invested in their lives. I was an assassin, it was my job to take lives, not save them, and somewhere along the lines that had gotten confused.

I wouldn't kill them. I couldn't. But I also wasn't going to keep coming to their rescue when they didn't need me to.

Now if only I could believe my own lies.

CHAPTER FOURTEEN

"THANK YOU, MARIBELLE," I SAID as I took my now-clean garments from the young maid.

"It was no problem. I'm more than happy to clean them whenever you need."

She smiled at me, and her genuine kindness shone through her eyes as she looked at me. I knew she wouldn't be able to see me through the hood of the cloak, but I had a feeling that she would be one of those rare enough not to be affected by the curse. While the men hadn't reacted, I didn't think that had anything to do with them being immune to it like I thought Maribelle was.

"I'm glad that I got to meet you," I told her honestly. "Anytime you need me, just call out my name, alright?"

Her face seemed to fall a bit, and I felt bad, even as I didn't understand why she was so upset.

"You're leaving?" She said, her tone as sad as her face now looked.

"I need to. There are some not very nice people after me, and I need to lead them away from the castle."

She nodded, her face clearing slightly.

"But you'll come back as soon as you take care of them," there was no doubt in her voice as she talked like killing people was something she saw me do every day.

"Well—"

"I'll see you soon," she said, interrupting me like I had done to the Prince earlier.

I couldn't help but smile at her, even if she couldn't see it.

"Remember," I said. "Call my name if—"

"I ever need help. Got it." She nodded, and I couldn't hold back the chuckle this time.

"Right." I nodded. "And thanks again."

Turning, I headed towards the door, clothing gathered up in my arms. I would change and leave the Princes clothes outside the door to be washed.

The feeling of having my own cloak and armor back on was a relief. It almost felt like I was finally able to take a full breath after years of struggling to breathe. There was nothing wrong with the Prince's clothes, except that I felt vulnerable while wearing them.

I had one last stop before leaving, and I found that the Prince must have already known I would be coming.

A note rested on top of the case holding my weapons.

'Don't worry Kitten, we'll see you soon. Until then, stay safe, and thank you for the invaluable information that you've provided us. I'm going to go over this intel with my father and see what we can do to *help lighten the burden I know this caused you.*

Yours, Prince Adair.'

A smile curled up my lips and I tucked the note into one of the many pockets lining my outfit. The Prince's scrawl was elegant, and I knew that I would enjoy rereading his note for years to come. Even if I thought he was wrong.

I wouldn't be back, no matter how much I might want to.

I didn't make it very far into the forest before I felt it.

Magic surged around me too fast for me to be able to escape. The trap snapped closed, and bands of magic closed around my body, binding my arms and legs closed tightly and causing me to fall to the ground like a log.

The breath was knocked from my lungs as I hit the ground, unable to catch myself. Figures came out through the trees, and I cursed myself for not paying better attention. My focus had been on my thoughts of the men I had just left instead of the forest around me, and now I was going to pay for my distraction.

"How kind of you to join us," one of the assassins said as they stepped forward.

He was newer to the guild, and the few times I had met him he had been kind to me. I had found it odd, but he hadn't seemed to have an ulterior motive. He was one of the few people of the guild I actually liked, so seeing him now was almost like a punch to the face.

He was also the one to warn me about the Prince, which was

another reason I was so shocked to see him here.

The Guild Master probably knew how I felt about the man, and that was why he had been sent. As I looked around at the other people gathered around me, I found that most of them were a few people I tolerated. Most of them had morals, though they weren't as rigid as mine. I liked them, and the Guild Master knew I wouldn't be able to kill them so easily.

Damn him.

I filtered through my options, trying to think of a way out that would leave their lives intact. I wasn't going to kill these people if I could avoid it. I had enough blood on my hands without killing some of the people I liked. Even if they didn't feel the same way.

"It's a pleasure to see you again, West," I said, and there was no sarcasm in my voice.

Something flashed across his face, and I saw his eyes flick to the others gathered around me. He couldn't seem to look at me and, while I wanted to think it was because he also liked me the slightest bit, I wasn't going to allow myself to wish for something that wasn't likely.

"What did you do to make the Guild Master want you dead so badly?" He asked me finally as all of the people gathered finally filtered into the clearing.

There was no way that I would be able to take all of them on and survive. Not to mention that ten of the people gathered were people I actually considered good people.

For assassins, at least.

"I failed to die the first time he tried to kill me," I said with a smile in my voice.

That made him pause, and I watched as his face shifted the slightest bit.

"What does that mean?" He asked, something in his voice I wasn't sure about.

I couldn't tell what he was thinking, but something told me he was honestly listening to what I had to say.

A little of my own magic was all that it took to break the magic binds that were holding me down, but instead of standing, I just sat facing him with my legs crossed. Those around me tensed, but I paid them no mind.

"I became a threat, and I refused to die when he sent me out on solo missions that required a team to complete." I said, playing with the foliage in front of me as I felt some of the others get into better positions to attack. "I hadn't done anything to deserve it then, but now..."

I let my voice trail off, and left it implied that I had done something to deserve this death sentence *now*.

Surprisingly, a smile came over West's face, and instead of attacking me, I felt his magic fade as he relaxed his posture.

"So, we weren't wrong," his voice was soft enough I almost didn't catch what he said.

But all his words did was confuse me. "What?"

"What are you doing, West?" One of the men behind me asked.

His tone was aggressive, and he was one of the men here I would have no problem killing. He was so far under the Guild Master's thumb that I could tell he was starting to enjoy killing others. He was fighting to rise in the ranks, and he didn't care what he needed to do to make it happen.

"I can tell you what I'm *not* doing," West said, joining me on the ground with his legs stretched out in front of him as he rested his weight on his arms. "I'm not going to kill her just because the Guild Master is scared that she's going to take over the guild. If I did that, then I would be on her shit list when she kicks all our asses and takes over the guild anyway."

"What?" Me and the man behind me said at the same time.

My voice was surprised, while his was angry.

I saw a few of the others shift on their feet, and the air seemed to grow more tense.

"What are you talking about, West?" I asked him, suddenly more tense than I was before.

"If the Guild Master is going to go after those he considers a threat, then there's nothing to stop him from taking us all out one by one. You aren't the only one he's gone after recently, and I'm not going to take out a friend just because he's nervous."

"A friend?" I asked him quietly.

It hadn't occurred to me that anyone in the guild could be my friend. Sure, I didn't hate all of them, and I genuinely liked West, but I hadn't ever thought I would have friends. It was a sad result of my upbringing, but I didn't see what I had to offer in a friendship.

"Of course, you're my friend," he said, sending me an amused smile. "And I'm not the only one that feels that way."

"We're aware that the Guild Master handpicked us because we share a bond of kinship that he knew you wouldn't be willing to destroy." One of the women standing to the side of me said, stepping closer. "It was obvious to everyone who you liked, and who you didn't."

My brow furrowed with concern. I hadn't thought my feelings had been so apparent. It was true I was kinder to those that I liked, but did that make us friends?

"It doesn't matter what you think," the man from behind me growled. "You were given an order from the Guild Master. We were told to bring her in, dead or alive."

"That is what we were ordered," West nodded, not making a move to attack me.

The man behind me growled, and the shift in magic let me know that he was starting to shift shape. He was a wolf shifter, and though he was more dangerous in his other form, he wasn't a true threat. Not in the way that West would have been if he had attacked me.

My head tilted to the side as I examined the man sitting in front of me. What did he have to gain from not attacking me? Or was this just a ploy to make me lower my guard so he could attack me when I was too tired to defend myself?

"Then, I'll just have to kill you both." The garbled words came out just before his shift finished and he lunged for my back.

Instead of drawing blood, all he did was tug on my cloak. It was impervious to most shifter's claws and teeth, something that hadn't actually taken much magic or effort to make happen.

He leapt back, and the others around me seemed to take that as their cue to attack. I finally got to my feet, but instead of joining the fight, I watched in confusion as the guild members turned on each other.

West stood up and came to stand beside me as I watched the people that I liked take down the other seven with ease. Shock and confusion flowed through me.

What...was happening?

"I'm not sure I understand what's happening here," I finally admitted to him softly.

"All you need to know, is that we're behind you. Whatever you choose to do. The Guild Master has been targeting more and more of his own agents, and I have a feeling that we would have been next. Aside from that, we all know that you've been taking some of the more dangerous missions in our place. You're our friend, and we noticed all the small things you were trying to do." He turned to me as the others moved closer to us. "There are more people in the guild than you know that are tired of the way things are being done. We may be assassins, but that doesn't mean we agree with the Guild Master's vile ways. He's become more and more corrupt as time goes on, and you're the only one that's powerful enough to take him down."

I frowned, not at all sure that was possible. He was extremely powerful, not to mention that he didn't have the same hesitations that I did. And he had a hold on me that I wasn't sure I could break.

"I don't know..." I let my voice trail off.

West reached up and tugged at the back of my hood, pulling it back just far enough that the spell hiding my face dispelled. I looked at him out of the corner of my eye, not sure what he was thinking, but not fighting his actions either.

There was no hatred or disgust in his gaze as he looked at me, but there was understanding. He knew about the curse, but it didn't affect him. I could feel my brows lower with confusion. None of the others around us attacked me either, instead they stood before us like they were waiting for something.

"You're odd," I said to West, the words escaping before I could stop them, and I felt a touch of pink on my cheeks.

He chuckled at me, and the others around us also laughed. It was an odd scene we made, dead bodies surrounding us while they laughed at my embarrassing words.

"Yes," West nodded, not denying my words. "Now, what would you like for us to do?"

His words surprised me, both the fact that he had agreed that he was odd and the fact that he expected me to tell him what to do.

"I'm not sure what you expect me to say," I told him honestly.

What did he want me to do? I wasn't going to order them around; I didn't like the idea of being responsible for so many lives. The list of people I needed to protect kept growing, and I wasn't sure how I was supposed to take care of them all. The pressure was familiar, though I hadn't thought about taking care of so many people since I was a child.

"Come on, boss lady," one of the others in the group said with a smile; his name was Charley. "You've lead teams before; this is no different."

I looked at him in surprise, the others around us nodding in agreement.

When did my life become so odd? This wasn't supposed to happen. I had never imagined something like this *could* happen. Not in a million years.

As I looked over those gathered around, something inside me shifted, my fear starting to fade. They were being sincere, there was no ulterior motive behind their actions.

My mind started to spin as I thought of a way to keep them all safe. They couldn't go back to the guild, I wouldn't sentence them to death, and if they were adamant on being part of my team, then that's exactly what would happen.

My team.

My allies.

My friends.

I would keep them safe.

All   of   them.

CHAPTER FIFTEEN

AS IT TURNED OUT, THIS GROUP of people was surprisingly easy to convince not to go back to the guild.

"We knew as soon as the Guild Master sent us out that we wouldn't be going back." West said as a few others disposed of the bodies. "You've got quiet the following at the guild. It's one of the reasons the Guild Master saw you as a threat."

The more West told me, the more mystified I had become. Apparently, I had more friends and allies than I thought. It was weird to me that these people liked me enough to follow me, but West assured me that it was true. I still wasn't sure what to believe, but he hadn't lied to me once during our conversation. That, more than anything was throwing me for a loop.

West was powerful. Extremely so. Between that and his charm I was sure that he would be the one that all these people chose to follow. I was still in a haze of disbelief as I looked at those gathered around us. Why were they here? They were putting their lives on the line by defying the Guild Master. And they were trusting me to keep them safe. They *wanted* to follow my orders, and not his.

I pinched the bridge of my nose as I tried to think about what to do. Now, it wasn't just the men at the castle that I needed to protect, but these guys as well. The other problem was that they weren't just going to be running from the Guild Master, but the nights of the kingdom. What had happened with me?

There was an unwritten rule that stated assassins didn't get to have friends, I was sure of it. But these people, along with the four I had just left in the castle, seemed determined to prove me wrong.

Getting caught in the castle should have been an instant death sentence, but the Prince had let me live. I wasn't sure that the same could be said of my new allies if they were to do the same. At the same time, I knew that if I asked them to do *nothing* they would go stir crazy. I was stuck between a rock and certain death.

How pleasant.

"By the way," West said, bringing my attention back to the group in front of me. "What *have* you been doing?"

My eyes ran over his face as I looked at him, the others around us going quiet as they waited to hear my answer. Would my answer change the way that they looked at me? Would they decide that I was more trouble than I was worth if I told them the truth?

Shaking those thoughts from my head, I sent West a smile. Either they would agree with my actions, or they wouldn't. It wasn't like their opinions would make me choose to do something different, and I wasn't going to stop protecting them even if they decided my actions made me unworthy of leading them.

"I was protecting him from the guild," I watched as his eyes widened in surprise, apparently not having expected that answer.

"Huh," he said as another smile covered his face. "And how did Adair like having your protection?"

It was my turn to be surprised, and I looked at him, really looked at the assassin standing before me. Wariness filled my being, and I started to doubt everything all over again. What did West really want with me? What were they all *really* doing here?

"You know the Prince?" I asked, taking a step back from him.

All my actions did was make his smile widen though, his amusement clear.

"Of course, he's the one that ordered me to join the guild," West was still smiling, but his words had completely thrown me off.

Adair had ordered him to join the guild? He knew the Prince? Did that mean all the people here knew about the Prince? Were they all working for him? All my thoughts started to race as I looked at those gathered around me in a new light.

I thought back, realizing that they had all joined after I was sent after the Prince the first time a few months ago. My mind flashed back to the Prince saying that they had done research on me and how much they had seemed to know. Was West feeding them information on me? Were they still here to keep an eye on me?

"Sneaky," I muttered. "Point to the Prince."

I hadn't expected him to send someone in to join the guild, but I should have. He wasn't dumb, though I certainly felt that way myself right now for not having thought this was something he would do.

West chuckled and I looked at him out of the corner of my

eye, not sure what to expect from him now.

"So, if you *were* protecting the Prince, what are you doing now?" He asked, the others were starting to wonder around, talking amongst themselves as the tension in the air faded completely.

"I may not have done anything to deserve being kill before, but now I've given the Prince everything he needs to dismantle the guild. That being said," I told him, watching as his eyes turned calculating. "I was going to lure the guild members out one by one and take them out before going after the Guild Master. I gave him the information on the off chance that I would fail."

"Smart," West said, his eyes turning with thoughts I couldn't read. "But, you're worried someone is going to try and make a play for him while your away."

His words weren't a question, and I nodded. Now that I was talking with him, something about West reminded me of being around the other three men. It was something I should have picked up on earlier. The same bond between us as the one I had with the others, and I realized that it was what had convinced me to believe his words.

"While I know that he can handle himself, I can't help but feel that something else is coming. There's a threat here that I can't see, and I'm not sure it has anything to do with the guild. Something else is happening behind the scenes, and I need to figure out what it is before it's too late."

"There have been whispers," West agreed, turning to look at me as some of the others wandered closer. "A group of lords aren't happy with the way things are going. The King has turned a blind eye to some of their misdoings until now, but the Prince isn't so lenient. With the King getting older there have been mutters of them trying to take the throne."

"And it's not just the lords of this kingdom either," the same female from earlier said.

Chelsea was her name, I remembered. She was a battle mage, and sneaky enough to give a shifter a run for their money.

"The bordering kingdom is going to try and make a claim for the throne to expand their territory." I said as I thought about what they were saying, and what I already knew.

"Not to mention the fae," Charley muttered.

"What?" I asked, my gaze zeroing in on him.

"It's just rumors and hearsay," he waved his hand, but that news unsettled me the most.

"So, we have lords of this kingdom and the next all planning to make a bid for the throne," I muttered, mind spinning. "If a challenge is put forth, then there's a chance that Adair would have to actually fight for what is rightfully his. But how are they planning to do that? The people love him, I've seen it. There's no way they are going to be able to turn all of them against the crown."

Still, something about this whole situation was bugging me.

The right of succession was passed down through the royal blood line. That meant that the Prince was the one that was next in line for the throne. It took a lot to call his rights to that into question. Either a majority of the people in the kingdom had to agree that he didn't deserve it, or all of the lords or council members had to agree.

Even then, he would be able to defend his right to rule. There would be a competition that would come into play that would decide the next ruler of the kingdom. There could be up to ten people that volunteer to take his place, and he would be able to fight for a chance to keep his title. He was guaranteed a spot in the competition.

Though it wasn't exactly a rule, it was unheard of that someone from another kingdom was nominated to take over. Especially a kingdom that we weren't friendly with.

It shouldn't have been possible that his right to rule would be called into question, but that didn't mean that it couldn't happen.

I needed to find out more.

"Ionia," West said, getting my attention. "What do you want us to do?"

"Do you agree that the Prince is the right person for this kingdom?" I asked him, and I knew that he understood what I was asking without me having to say it.

"I'll help him, and you." He nodded.

Some of the tension fell away from me and my shoulders relaxed. My gaze moved over those gathered, and they all nodded their heads one by one. The Prince was well liked, even by those of the assassin's guild.

Lucky him.

"Right," I nodded, thinking quickly about a way to protect him and keep the guild away. "We need more information about what's happening."

Looking around at the people with me, I thought about their skills and what would work best without putting them in danger.

"I need someone to watch the nobles and the people of this country and our neighboring countries as well. West," I turned to him as six of the ten people branched off when I pointed to them. "I would like to ask you to guard the Prince while I whittle down the remaining guild members."

"It would be my pleasure," he said, a smile on his face.

"You four are to accompany him and do as he asks," I pointed to the remaining four people.

"Yes, Guild Master," The chanted at once, and I paused in shock.

Guild master...That hadn't been expected at all.

"I'm not—"

"It's either that or just master, but we know how you feel about that," West said with a cheeky smile.

"I have a name, you know." I grumbled at him as the others watched on with amusement.

"And it's lovely, but when it comes to work, I'm going to use your title. I respect you, and I want you to know it."

The others nodded in agreement with his words, and I muttered at them all under my breath.

"See you soon, Guild Master." And with his final words, West turned and ran off towards the castle, the others following.

"Point to West," I said, but I couldn't stop the smile that slid over my face.

Pulling my hood back over my face and making sure the spell that hid my features was once again active, I turned and started in the direction of the guild hall.

The others were skilled; they would get their jobs done.

Now, it was my turn.

It had been three weeks since we had made our plans, and things had been troublingly quiet. There had only been one attempt on the Prince's life, but West and his team had easily been able to quash it.

No helpful information had been brought in by my spies, but there was a lead that I had sent them out to follow up on. Tensions throughout the kingdom had been rising, and we still weren't sure where it was coming from.

I had also gotten news that the King was sick.

He had arrived back from his travels and shortly after had fallen ill. The fact that someone, *something*, as powerful as him had taken ill didn't bode well for us. I may not have liked the King much, but he was still the Prince's father, and some part of me wanted to comfort Adair.

But I hadn't been too lucky, either.

Another hit landed in my gut. I was exhausted, and while I still had the majority of my magic, using it would bring much more unsavory people to me. The Guild Master hadn't wasted time in sending his members after me.

Team after team had come at me, not leaving me time to rest or heal. I hadn't slept in more than five days. I hadn't eaten in almost as long, and water breaks were few and far between. It felt like I had fought everyone in the guild by now, but I knew that wasn't the case at all.

Surprisingly, I had found more companions that wanted to join West and I among my attackers. I had almost twenty assassins now, and it still surprised me that they were willing to go against the Guild Master.

My distraction cost me, and another kick landed, this time sending me to the ground. My world spun as the force made me roll. Panting, I finally stopped and made my tired body climb to one knee. Three men and one woman surrounded me, a pile of bodies surrounding us. I was covered head to toe in blood, most of it not my own.

"Just give up and *die* already," the current team leader I was facing growled.

He brought up a ball of fire, throwing it at me, only for it to hit me and fizzle out without doing anything but giving me an energy boost. Fire was *mine* to control, not his.

"Never," I spat at him, blood from my cut lip escaping as well.

I raised a hand, vines growing from the ground to surround one of his companions. I listened to his screams as he struggled futilely to escape. His struggles soon ceased, but the small bit of magic had cost me.

Panting breaths escaped me, and I was too slow to avoid the kick aimed at me. It hit my shoulder, the sound of a snap ringing out as my collarbone snapped at the force. I hissed at the sharp pain.

Sending a fire ball at the man running at me, he hollered in pain, not having the same affinity for fire as his leader. He burned up in seconds, and I took another kick to the stomach.

I was exhausted, and I needed to end this quickly and leave the area before someone else could come. I had been pinned down for too long. I didn't sense anyone else in the area aside from these two, and I was going to take advantage of that.

The woman bared her fangs at me, and I growled right back at her. Anger and frustration were riding me hard, and the need to take that out on her was overwhelming.

My body didn't want to respond to my commands, but I forced myself to pull my feet under me, pulling a weapon from my body that grew into a spear. My arm whipped back and launched the weapon too fast for even her speed to avoid. Using the wind to aid my aim and make it go even faster.

She went down with a thump, and I cried out with frustrated

pain as something sharp entered my side from behind.

My vision flickered, my once injured eye flickering between black and white and color. Something that hadn't happened since the first time I had regained my vision after it was injured.

It flickered again as I turned on my last opponent, and what I saw made me hesitate. While the surrounding area was black and white, the man had a red glow surrounding him, black specks interwoven throughout.

The dual vision made me sick and dizzy, not allowing me to stop him as he reached out. He grabbed my throat and used his strength to lift me to my feet. I was lighter than a human, something that hadn't ever been a problem, until now.

I had no doubt that if I was as heavy as a human he wouldn't have been able to lift me so high, or hold me so far from his body that I wasn't able to get the right leverage to make him let go.

My hands wrapped around his forearm as I tried to release some of the pressure along my windpipe. It wasn't working, and instead of the flickering black and white, my vision just started to fade completely.

This couldn't be it; this couldn't be the way that I died.

I hadn't done any of the things that I needed to. I hadn't taken down the Guild Master, or made sure that my people and the men at the castle were safe. I still had things that I needed to accomplish.

Releasing one of my hands, I reached into my cloak and pulled one of my weapons, my hands fumbling around before I could get a good enough grasp. Using the last of my strength, I manipulated the weapon, and swung, aiming for the man's throat.

For a moment nothing happened, and both my arms fell

175

uselessly to my sides, all my strength gone. Then all at once, the man's grasp released from my throat and I fell to the ground beside his body.

I just laid there, panting as I watched the life fade from his eyes.

I knew that I needed to leave this area, knew that I had to find somewhere to hide and rest, but my body was too tired to move. Whether I wanted it or not, I was going to pass out, and I could only hope that no one else came along before I was able to defend myself.

CHAPTER SIXTEEN

"IONIA!"

The sound of a woman's scream reverberated through my head, and I jerked up to sitting, my body protesting even that small movement.

There was no one here, but the sound of my name rang out once again.

"Ionia!"

The sound was filled with terror, and when I recognized it, I snarled.

Maribelle was in trouble, and she needed me.

My power swirled around me, and for this brief moment all my pain and exhaustion faded away. I had made a promise to Maribelle, one that she didn't understand, and whether it killed me or not, my magic was going to make sure I fulfilled it.

Faster than ever before, the wind and my own magic forced my tired body to move in the direction my friend was calling to me from.

"Ionia!" She tried to call me again, and I cursed the fact that I was so far away when I heard the tears in her voice.

I pushed myself as hard as I could, using the magic and wind to push my body even faster than before.

The journey, that should have taken an entire day, wasn't going to take me more than twenty minutes. I only hoped that wasn't too long.

Fear filled me when Maribelle's voice went silent. I was less than a minute out, and I knew that as soon as she was safe, I would pay for what I had done to get here.

"Ionia!" West called in surprised as I ran past him.

I didn't pause, didn't even pay attention as he started after me, his own abilities allowing him to keep up.

"Hey, Ionia, what's wrong?" He tried again.

I leapt the fence, my body knowing where to go even if I wasn't sure where she was. I grunted, and slowed as I got closer, the guards raising an alarm as their eyes finally registered my presence.

"Alert the Prince!"

"Intruders!"

Multiple cries rang out, but I didn't bother with them. Maribelle needed me.

I ran out behind the stables where my magic was pulling on me hardest, the sight before me making a growl come from my throat and my magic briefly flared up. There was a purple flash that surrounded me for a moment before I leapt at one of the men standing over a beaten and bloodied Maribelle.

He went down easily enough. West took down the second one while I finished off the third, none of the men having enough time to realize we were here before they were dead. Adrenaline was running through me so fast I was sure my heart was going to burst out from my ribs.

Maribelle was staring up at me with fear until she realized who I was. She was in pretty bad shape as she lay on the ground behind the barn, her clothing ripped to shreds. It looked like I had gotten here in time, but I still cursed that I hadn't gotten here sooner.

"Ionia?" She asked, and I realized that my body was swaying as the adrenaline and magic started to fade.

"Hey," West said softly, taking a step closer to me as Maribelle finally noticed him. "What happened?"

My strength was fading as the magic that allowed me to act faded with the remainder of my energy. My wounds made their presence known, the sound of steps echoing with the pain throughout my body.

"Hello, West," I said, my voice breathless. "I'm glad your safe Maribelle."

"Ionia!" They both cried out as my legs collapsed, blood seeping from my side as it failed to heal.

I didn't have enough energy, and my advance healing was failing to kick in.

Guards turned the corner, but my view of them blocked when West and Maribelle leaned over me, calling my name.

"Don't worry," I told them. "It's only a scratch."

Tears poured down Maribelle's face as she apologized like this was her fault. West's eyes were focused on me, a snort releasing from his chest at my attempted humor.

"Idiot, what did you do? *Let* them almost kill you?" His words were teasing, but his hands were gentle as he looked me over, concern written on his face.

The guards moved to surround us, pulling weapons, and pointing them in our direction. My protective urges kicked in, but I wasn't able to do more than shift my body. Especially after West pressed down on my shoulders, making me hiss in pain as he encouraged me to lie still.

"Who are you? What are you doing here?" One of the guards asked as he stepped forward, blade directed at West.

He snorted but ignored the man as he pulled at the button that held my cloak closed. My hand rose to grab his when he tried to push it from my shoulders.

"Now isn't the time; we need to get a look at your wounds," he grunted at me, easily pushing my hands off and making me glared when he pushed my cloak away.

The spells hiding my body and face from view faded, but I was too tired to put up much of a fight. A few of the men surrounding us shifted, but none of them came after us. A welcome surprise.

"Wait," One of the guards whispered. "I think I recognize her."

They started to mutter under their breath to each other, but they didn't lower their weapons.

"Oh, Ionia, what happened?" Maribelle asked, her hands over her mouth as she looked at me with horror.

"I told you," I smiled at her, pushing myself to a sitting position with West's help. "It's just a scratch, I'll be fine."

And though some of the wounds were deadly, if nothing else happened, my words wouldn't be a lie. I would be fine. It was just going to be a long and painful recovery.

A noise that sounded like a roar sounded out from somewhere near the castle, and though the sound should have scared me, it offered comfort instead. West chuckled as the guards shifted with unease.

"Looks like Adair hasn't changed much."

His easy use of the Prince's first name made some of the guards around us shift on their feet.

"You know the Prince?" Maribelle asked softly, trying to distract herself.

"Sorry that it took me so long to get here, Maribelle," I apologized to her softly.

Her lip trembled, and seemingly forgetting about both of our injuries she lunged and wrapped her arms around my waist, her head leaning against my broken collar bone. My instinct was to fling her away from me, but instead I wrapped my own arms tightly around her, offering her all the comfort that I could while she cried out her terror at what had just happened. The pain was intense, and I tilted my head down into her hair, biting my tongue as I fought the urge to scream.

I felt one of the guard's step closer with his blade at the ready. West stood, moving to stand in front of us in a fighting stance. Maribelle squeezed me tighter, unaware of what was happening around her, and I lost my breath as I felt my face drain of color. A small sound of pain escaped me, and though Maribelle didn't hear it over the sound of her own sobs, West did, and I heard him release a sound of frustration.

"What's going on here?" A loud voice called out.

A loud, *familiar* voice.

"Sir, we've surrounded the intruders that made it onto the castle grounds and sent someone to inform the Prince." One of the men informed Xavier.

"Who are you, and what are you doing here?" Xavier questioned tiredly as I heard him step closer.

My whole body was shaking with pain and emotion at his presence. It had only been a few weeks, but I had missed them. It was strange and having West at my back was strangely reassuring.

West stayed silent, and I heard Xavier move as another, more foreboding presence continued to come closer. It wasn't Xavier, though I knew he was dangerous in his own right.

The Prince was coming, and I didn't know whether to laugh, cry, or *run*.

It was too bad I wasn't sure I could do anything but sit here.

"Move," the Prince demanded as he made his way around the corner, a growl in his voice.

"Adair?" Xavier questioned.

"Lower your weapons," the Prince demanded stepping around his men. "Tell the infirmary to get a bed ready at once."

I didn't hear anyone moving, and West tensed up at my back, his leg resting against me to let me know he was here.

"Now!" The Prince roared, and everyone but Xavier, Merrick, and the three of us scattered.

Maribelle shuddered in my arms, and I slowly released her, my breaths still coming in pants of pain.

"It will be okay," I told her, my voice hoarse with pain. "Go to Merrick, he can help you, alright?"

She nodded, unsure, but trusting me enough that she stood and shakily walked over to where I could sense the mage was standing.

"What are you doing here, West?" Xavier asked quietly, and the man behind me shrugged.

"Just following orders," he responded with a light chuckle.

I just sat there for a moment, trying to get my pain and breathing under control, leaning more and more of my weight against West's leg.

He reached a hand back to rest against the top of my head, his warmth bringing comfort as my eyes started to flutter.

"Kitten?" Adair asked softly, stopping a good distance back as he waited for me to respond. "Are you okay?"

West was relaxed now, and I was surprised about that with the three powerhouses surrounding us.

"No, Prince," I croaked, my vision starting to fade. "I'm not."

My body went weightless as I started to slump to the side, consciousness leaving me as the pain and my wounds finally overwhelmed my system.

"You were supposed to get information and protect her West, not let her almost die," the Prince's growl was the first thing I heard as I woke up.

West grunted from close to my side, and I forced my eyes open.

"I was doing my job, Addy," West said, making the Prince growl.

I snickered at the nickname, the teasing in West's voice clear.

"I like that one, Addy." My voice was still hoarse, and my body was still achy, but I could tell that most of my worst injuries were healed.

"Don't encourage him," the Prince groaned, but there was a measure of relief in his voice as well.

"He's an insufferable ass as it is," Merrick agreed with a chuckle.

I opened my eyes to find that I was surrounded by all four men, all of them looking worn and worried. The room must have been in the medical ward. Either that, or a torture chamber.

"I find his presence soothing," I said, the words sneaking out before I could stop them.

Gold flashed through the Prince's eyes, but West just chuckled.

"I'm glad you enjoy being around me," the man in question said.

"Well," I said, sitting up and shaking my head to try and dispel the rest of the cloudiness from my head. "I wouldn't go that far."

Xavier snorted and leaned back in his chair.

"What happened, Kitten?" The Prince asked quietly, the humor draining from the room.

My smile faded as I thought about what had happened over the last few days.

"I almost failed, that's what happened."

West sucked in a breath, and the others exchanged careful looks.

"Failed at what?" Merrick asked.

"How many?" West asked at the same time.

I closed my eyes and leaned my head down to rest in my hands, my collar bone barely protesting.

"Forty-eight, give or take a few," I said, trying to think back over the past few days and counting the tally of bodies I had left behind.

West cursed and stood, running a hand through his hair.

"You're lucky to be alive," he said, turning to face me as a slight glow encompassed his hands. "You should have called on us to help. Idiot!"

"I didn't have the time," I growled right back closing my eyes when my vision started to flash again. "I barely had time to breath. Don't you dare berate me when you don't know what happened."

Taking a breath, the glow around his hands faded, the others looking back and forth between us.

"You're right. I'm sorry, Guild Master," his voice was calmer, but there was still frustration there.

"Guild master?" Xavier asked, and I growled again.

"I'm too tired to deal with you right now," I said, looking away from all of them, then trying, and failing to get out of the medical bed.

"Yeah, that's not going to happen," Merrick said, his magic gently coming to wrap around me and forcing me to lay back down.

I gave in, panting with the effort the brief fight against him had cost me.

"You are nowhere near ready to be standing. West, if you can't stop antagonizing her, you're going to have to leave." Merrick's voice was hard, and he looked at the other two in the room as well. "That goes for you two as well. She can tell us what happen after she's healed."

My eyes were starting to get heavy again, and I couldn't tell if it was Merrick, or my own body that was trying to make me sleep this time.

"Your right," West agreed with a sigh. "I'm sorry, Ionia."

I nodded, not bothering to open my eyes. It took too much effort.

"Your team?" I asked him softly.

"Still on patrol. The castle's safe."

"Good," I said, falling back into a healing sleep.

The phantom feeling of a warm hand pressed against the top of my head.

CHAPTER SEVENTEEN

WHEN I WOKE UP NEXT, it was to find that my clothes had been washed and I was alone in the Prince's bed. There was a vague memory of Maribelle coming in and helping me change. I didn't remember much, but I did remember scolding her for being out of bed herself.

I ran my hands over my face as I sat up, thinking about everything that had happened, and everything I still had left to do. The Guild Master was still out there, and I had only dealt with half the guild members. There was still too many for me to feel good about allowing the situation to continue to get worse. I couldn't linger here.

My body was still weak as I got out of bed, but I wasn't in pain any longer. I really needed to figure out what they did that helped me heal as fast as I had been. My natural healing ability was fast, but not even I could heal all the damage I had sustained in one night.

My internal clock let me know that it had only been a few hours since I had gone to sleep, and I was relieved that not much time had passed. I needed to check on Maribelle, and then check in with West and see what else had happened since the last time we had been in contact a week ago. I also needed to let him know who I had taken care of at the guild.

If we could figure out who I still had left to deal with, it would make it easier to predict what actions they would take. Not to mention we would have a better idea of which abilities they had. It would make it easier to go on the offense, and not just wait for them to come for me.

Granted, that had been the original plan, but I hadn't expected the Guild Master's desperation. And that's what I was going to assume this was.

Something about all of this was off, but I couldn't think of anything that would cause him to come after me this hard. Unless he knew what I had been up to, that is. Sure, I was powerful, but until recently, I hadn't gone against his wishes. He had taken me in when I was younger, and even now, knowing that I needed to take him out, there was a part of me that was sad that the man that raised me was going to have to die by my hand.

He wasn't a father by any means, more a jailer, but he had allowed me to live there while I grew. He had trained me to take care of myself. Despite the fact that I had a curse placed on me, he had been able to work past it and allow me to live in the guild hall.

Even knowing it wasn't out of the kindness of his heart, I couldn't quite hate him as much as I should have.

Sighing, I forced myself up, looking down at the nightgown I was wearing with horror. What was this? Why did they dress me in something so...delicate?

I didn't like how vulnerable this outfit made me feel. I ripped it over my head, and winced when the fabric tore because of my enthusiasm. Quickly dressing, I picked the fabric up and looked at the tear I had caused.

"What happened?"

I looked up to see the Prince leaning against the doorway with a smile on his face.

I winced. "Sorry, guess I got to excited. I'll pay you for it,"

Though, I didn't know how, all the money I had earned was stashed at the guild. I had spent all my nights living off the land, something that was easy considering I was a trained huntress and killer. Not that that would help with fixing or paying for the garment in my hands.

The Prince laughed at me and shook his head.

"I told her you wouldn't like it, but she insisted it would be better for your injuries. It's the first time Maribelle has stood up to anyone, so I didn't want to argue with her about it." He sent me a smirk as he continued. "We'll just pretend it got lost in the wash."

"But, she does the washing..." I said.

"I know," was his chuckled response.

He was letting me off the hook, and without any money to pay him back, I was going to have to take the out.

"Alright," I nodded. "Where's West?"

His eyes flashed gold, but I didn't get the sense that he was particularly angry. Though I wasn't sure what emotion he was feeling at the moment.

"He's with Xavier, going over the documents you created for us," the Prince said, surprising me. "They're in one of conference rooms."

I nodded, pulling my hood up and walking out into the hall when he gestured me out.

The fact that West could read the parchment told me that the Prince and the others trusted him completely. Something in me had doubted that the Prince had really sent someone into an assassin's guild, but he was basically confirming that they had some sort of connection.

Curiosity rose inside me as I wondered how they had met. All the intel I had been able to gather on him and his companions made me think it had always been just the three men. And I hadn't seen him at all while I had been observing the Prince.

That made me nervous to think about. Was I losing my touch? Or was he a lot better than I had given him credit for? The fact that I considered him the best and most dangerous person from the guild already made me wary.

How did I miss him? And how was I going to keep my guard up around these four men that seem to get below my skin? They were all able to sneak up on me to an extent, something that had never happened before. I had gotten better, but the Prince was still too quiet on his feet, and if he wasn't upset, I couldn't sense him coming until it was too late.

"You should get him a bell," I muttered, forgetting for a moment that the Prince was walking beside me.

He chuckled. "It wouldn't help. It's a benefit of being what I am, though you always seem to sense my presence just fine."

He looked down at me, his curiosity clear. I turned to look up into his face, knowing that he couldn't see me biting my lip. Or, I hoped he couldn't since I had enhanced the spell.

"Maybe, but not quickly enough for it to help anything," I told him.

"Do you think I would hurt you?" His face was blank, his tone only sounding curious, but there was a weight to the air that made me think my answer was important to him.

"I don't know you well, any of you, really. But, I don't think you would harm me intentionally, not at this point. That doesn't mean you're the only person that I need to be worried about though. If you are able to get the drop on me, then who's to say that someone else won't be able to? It's not you that I fear, but the thought I won't be quick enough when a true threat comes for me."

His eyes turned gold, and there was a slight sheen to his skin for a second while he seemed to process his thoughts.

"We'll work on it," and with those words, he faced forward, a troubled look on his face.

I wasn't sure what I had just done, but I had a feeling the Prince was upset. Only, I wasn't sure if he was upset with me, or *for* me. It was hard to tell, and I didn't have the best experience with people.

The hall we were walking through was more densely populated, and I slowed to walk just slightly behind the Prince, watching all the people as we passed.

He chuckled under his breath. "I thought you didn't want the job as my bodyguard,"

His words were teasing, and I smiled at him in return from under my hood.

"I don't, I'm just using you as a human shield like you suggested earlier."

He shook his head, a smile still on his face.

"You're willing to shut yourself in a room you know is about to explode, but a handful of people you could easily kill is enough to scare you."

"Hey!" I said, lightly smacking his arm and receiving a glare of disapproval from some of the women walking past us. "I can't just kill everyone that I walk past, that would make the

Prince angry. I've heard he's a beast of a man, you know."

"Yeah, I've heard he's a royal pain in the ass," the Prince agreed with a nod.

"On that fact, we can agree," I said solemnly.

He turned to look at me, chuckling. He reached out and wrapped an arm around my neck and pulled me close while he still walked on. I let out a squawk of disapproval, almost tripping over my own feet.

"Cheeky woman," he said, ignoring the curious gazes of those we passed.

"You're the one who said it, I just agreed." I said, fixing my cloak when he finally released me.

"True enough," he said, still smiling. "Maybe I was fishing for compliments."

"And maybe I think that your ego is big enough already," I said, dodging his reach this time, laughing as I bounced down the hall backward so I could see him.

"You're going to regret those words," He mock-threatened.

"Maybe," I agreed, though I wasn't worried in the least.

Turning, I grabbed the hand that was about to plunge a blade into my side just before it could make contact. The blank-eyed man winced, and I sighed as he finally dropped the blade. One of the women beside us stopped, her mouth opening like she was going to scream.

"Don't scream," I told her, my voice coming out sounding like music. "Everything is fine; it was a test."

She nodded, her mouth shutting as she continued on her way. A warm hand came down to rest on my shoulder, and I finally released the young man's wrist, lifting my hand to smack him in the forehead with my palm.

His eyes cleared instantly, a look of confusion taking over his features.

"Thank you for letting us know," I said, the Prince squeezing briefly before he removed his hand.

"Yes," Adair agreed. "I appreciate the forewarning."

"Oh," the young man said, his confusion clear. "I...you're welcome, I guess..."

Stepping over the blade to hide it, I watched him walk away, rubbing at his forehead like he was trying to remember what had just happened.

Using air, I lifted the blade under my cloak until it came to rest on my palm. Walking a little farther down the hall, the Prince followed me as I entered a room, shutting the door behind himself.

"You can come out now," I spoke, unconsciously putting my body between the threat and the Prince that was standing behind me.

A man stepped out into the open, the third and final son of the Guild Master. Though he was the least powerful of the three, his ability worked when his target came into view, no touching or bleeding required, just like his father. The effects didn't last nearly as long as his old man's, but that didn't make him any less dangerous.

"You shouldn't have turned on us, Ionia." Barth said. "Dad took you in, treated you like you were one of his own. How could you betray him like this?"

I tilted my head to the side, not feeling any indication that he was trying to use his ability on me. Curious.

"That man was nothing more to me than a dictator who tried to mold me into a weapon he could control,"

To be honest that was how he treated most of the guild

members, though he didn't raise most of them.

The Prince shifted behind me, and I only had a split seconds warning to step to the side. Sharp talon like claws swiped over where I had just been standing, and I turned to look up at the Prince's blank eyes.

Sighing, I took a step back as he aimed another swipe for my throat. He wasn't moving nearly as fast as I knew he could, letting me know that he was still somewhat aware of what was happening.

It was impressive, as not many people could fight off the effects of Barth's abilities. And though he was under the spell, I easily batted away his next attack.

"How rude, Adair. It's not nice to attack your friends," I stepped into his reach, lifting a hand and smacking my palm against his forehead, using a little more magic than before to ensure Barth's control wouldn't get another hold on him.

I let out a startled yelp when his arm came around my waist, holding me to him as his eyes cleared. The speed made my hood fall back and our gazes met. He held me to him tighter, his eyes not leaving my own for a second.

"You're right, that was rude of me," his voice was soft, and I felt captivated by his gaze, unable to look away.

"Is this why you left us? So you could try and get into the Prince's pants?" Barth said with disgust.

"I've already been inside his pants," I said, knowing he was speaking about an act much more intimate than borrowing the Prince's clothing.

"You disgusting little wretch," Barth spit, finally starting to walk closer to us as the Prince buried his face in my shoulder, his laughter making his whole body shake.

The assassin ran at us, bringing up a blade to attack while I was still being held in the Prince's arms. Yet, despite the fact we were about to be harmed, I wasn't anxious in the least.

Fast enough that even I had trouble tracking the movement, the Prince lifted his hand and grabbed Barth's face. Then, without even lifting his head from my shoulder, flames poured from his hands. Heat radiated from beside me, thought the flames didn't burn. Within seconds Barth was nothing but a pile of ash.

Lowering his hand, little embers fluttered about the room before going out. There was no trace of the final son of the Guild Master left behind.

"Huh," I said, the Prince finally lifting his head to look down at me with a smile. "Guess your convenient to keep around. Good to know."

Shaking his head, the Prince finally released me, taking his body heat with him, and causing me to shiver even though I wasn't cold.

"Yes, I guess I'm good for *something*."

"Hey," I said, pushing past him and into the hall. "Trash disposal is a very important job."

He laughed again, following me into the whisper-filled hall as I continued on my way to the room I could sense the others were gathered in.

"I guess it is," he said, humoring me.

I looked at him over my shoulder before my eyes widened. My hand rose to touch my head, my hood not pulled up to cover my face. I couldn't believe I had forgotten to bring it back up. I had never been so thoughtless before.

My hands reached to grab at the missing hood, but the Prince stopped them. Reaching around me with his other hand he opened the door I was now standing in front of.

That wasn't like me; I didn't forget things like pulling my hood up. The consequences were too severe.

Though...

I looked back down the hall still filled with people, and none of them were gazing at me with anger or disgust. At least, none that were doing so because of the curse. The Prince pushed me gently into the room where the others were waiting, ignoring my confused concern.

I wasn't sure what was happening but there was a part of me, a very small part, that felt something I wasn't sure I had felt since I was a child.

Hope.

CHAPTER EIGHTEEN

"SORRY TO KEEP YOU WAITING, I was put in charge of garbage disposal," Adair said as he dragged me farther into the room.

I smiled, not able to help myself at the Prince's teasing tone and the other's confused looks.

"Right..." Merrick said looking between us for a moment longer before turning back to the table he was sitting at.

The room wasn't too large, but there was a table surrounded by chairs, and the parchment that I had written was spread out across the top of it. I winced at the fear that rose up in me with the thought of the Guild Master finding out what I had done. Right now, he was only saying that I had betrayed him, he didn't believe that I could have done something like this. He was too sure of the power he held over those of the guild. Me included.

But, I should have been stronger. I was planning to take his life, so I shouldn't have feared his reaction to learning about my betrayal. Though a lifetime of conditioning wouldn't go away overnight. It had been much easier to write out the details of how the guild worked when I had thought I would be sentenced to death. Then I wouldn't have been here to deal with the consequences.

I didn't regret writing it down, not really. But there was the thought in the back of my mind that I wouldn't be the one that came out on top when we fought, and that part of me was terrified of what would happen to these men that I had just sentenced to death.

I couldn't let it happen. I needed to take the Guild Master out before he could find out about what I had done here.

"I think we need to talk about this information, and your reason for giving it to us," the Prince said, gently pushing me to a seat at the table before pulling it out and gesturing to the chair.

What should have been a gentlemanly move almost felt like a threat when put with his words. I hesitated before finally deciding to sit. While I was healed, I was still sore and tired. It didn't have anything to do with the fact that I wanted to sit beside them. Not at all.

"I thought somebody should have it, and you guys seemed the least likely to tell the Guild Master where you got it," I said with a shrug, the move feeling odd with my hood down.

My fingers twitched to pull it up, but the Prince was watching me intently, and I had a feeling he wouldn't appreciate me hiding my face. Little did he know I was a master of lying. Or twisting my words when it suited me. I hadn't always worn a hood, and you didn't grow up the way I did without learning to hide your thoughts and feelings.

"I don't think that's the full story," Merrick said, leaning back and watching me like the Prince.

I tilted my head to the side as I watched him, and I saw something like unease flash across his face. That brief flash of emotion made something inside my chest clench, and I lowered my gaze to the papers before us as I pushed my hurt away.

He had every right to be wary of me, I was an assassin that had threatened his life more than once.

A grunt came from the mage and my gaze jerked up to find him also looking at the parchment. Though there was an expression of pain on his face and a satisfied smile on West's.

I narrowed my eyes at the assassin, my vision flickering again so fast that it almost made me dizzy. He was in full color one minute, and the next he was glowing gold while the room faded to black and white. It was nauseating, and I needed to figure out what was happening so I could get a grip on whatever it was.

My eyes closed as I swallowed hard, my stomach slowly settling as I took a deep breath. When I opened them again it was to find all the men in the room watching me. Ignoring the odd occurrence for now, I focused on the task at hand.

Standing, I shuffled through the papers on the table until I found a few sheets that contained a list of names. Grabbing one of the writing utensils on the table, I started to look over them, crossing out the names of those I knew were dead, then handing it to West to go over. He took it without question, going through and removing the names of those he had dealt with as well. Curiously, he added a name and ability. I would have to look over the list when he was done again.

Once he was done, he placed them in a new pile between us, and we switched again. I grunted when I realized the names he added were people I had missed, and not new members. I had gotten sloppy, slipped up, and if he hadn't been here, I might have missed them. Luckily, two of the three names he had added were already dealt with.

"Sloppy," I muttered, forcing my mind to sharpen as I went

through my memories again, making sure that I hadn't missed anyone else.

"When did you take care of Barth?" West asked as he went over the lists a final time, the others watching on curiously.

"About five minutes ago," I said, causing him to raise a brow at me. "Though it was the Prince that took care of that piece of trash."

I gestured over at the Prince who was leaned back in his chair, looking at me through half open eyes. The way he was leaning back would make others think he was relaxed, but I could feel the tension and readiness, like lighting just under his skin. He was a predator on the hunt for his prey, and patience would ensure that he captured it.

The worst part was that I was fairly sure I was the prey; I just didn't know why he was hunting me.

"So, with this information, it's safe to assume that at least half of the guild is out of commission or dead. Better yet, it looks like there were more than I thought that wanted to get out from under the Guild Master. That will give us an advantage when we go after him." West's words made my eyes flick up to look at his face.

"There is no *we*," my voice came out sharper than I had intended, and I made a conscious effort to soften it when I spoke next. "I'm the one that will be taking out the Guild Master, you guys aren't going to go near him."

"Then, what was the point of giving us this information?" Xavier said, his voice almost sounding petulant.

"This was so you guys could better defend yourselves against him when he sent out more people to take your lives."

It was only a half-truth, but better than nothing.

"What you meant to say, was that this was in case you died

before you could take him out, correct?" The Prince was still watching me through his half-lidded gaze, but his words were almost cold.

I narrowed my eyes at him, not appreciating his tone, even if the words were true enough.

"Don't think that being royalty means you get to speak to me as if I'm an idiot. You don't know anything about me, not really, and you don't get to judge my actions."

My tone was fire to his ice, and he slowly sat up, his large form blocking out some of the light when he seemed to lean closer to me.

"So, I was right then? You weren't planning on making it back to us alive."

A small thrill ran through me, but it wasn't exactly fear. Though I didn't know what it was.

My vision flickered again, and the image of a large creature crouched over the Prince glowed purple, matching the color of the light surrounding him. I wasn't sure why this was happening now, but the large winged creatures image confirmed what I had been thinking about the Prince for some time now. Eventually the flickering became too much, and I had to take a deep breath as I fought a wave of nausea.

"What's going on with you today?" Merrick asked me softly as his eyes seemed to look through me. "Your magic is fluctuating like crazy, but it doesn't feel like you have control of it."

I frowned at him, wondering what he was seeing, but not wanting to seem weak by asking. At least his words had confirmed one thing for me: this vision, whatever it was, was my own magic at work, and wasn't something someone was doing to me. That was both good and bad; good because I would be able to learn to control it, but bad because I wasn't sure what had triggered the new ability, and that was going to be a problem.

"I'm fine," I told him, and when he opened his mouth to argue, I continued to speak over him. "It's none of your concern."

"But whatever is affecting you *is* our concern. You're one of us now, that means that whatever is going on with you is our responsibility as well." Xavier said, after Merrick's mouth snapped shut with a click.

A storm of emotions swirled through me, and for some reason rage was at the forefront. Opening my mouth, it was me that was interrupted this time.

"There's no use arguing," West said, looking at his fingers while he spoke like he didn't have a concern in the word. "They've made up their minds, so you won't be able to change them. This is what they do: they adopt the lost causes like us and make us like it."

There was something in his tone that made me think he had tried and failed to escape their grasp. My emotions seemed to calm as curiosity rose inside me. What had happened that made someone as powerful as West cave to their offer of companionship?

"Face it, Guild Master, you've unwittingly joined a group that's very exclusive, and there isn't a way to get out of it." There was a smirk on his face this time as his eyes finally came up to meet my own.

"I refuse to believe I have no control over those I choose to associate with. Besides," I said, standing to gather all the papers and put them back into some semblance of order. "I have a feeling something's coming, and you guys need to be worrying about yourselves."

That made West sit up straighter, the others noticing his

actions and taking his cue that something important was about to happen.

"What's going on?" Xavier asked, all thought of joking gone from his face.

"I don't have all the information yet, but it seems our suspicions are proving to be more true than not. I'm not sure when they are going to make their move, or who it is just yet, but the neighboring kingdom is involved." I told West, his face worried. "I was able to confirm that they are expecting something to happen, and I think it's going to happen soon."

"What's going to happen?" Merrick asked, his own magic seeming to add pressure to the already tense atmosphere.

"I don't think your father is sick through natural causes," I told Adair as I looked at him, a mix of emotions passing through his eyes. "But, I also think it's too late to stop what's been put into motion, even if we can find a cure to what ails him."

His lips compressed into a thin line as the other three looked at him with concern.

"So, it is a curse then," he said softly to himself.

"That, or some sort of poison. But I'm not sure he has much time left. Less if whoever is behind this has their way."

His eyes closed as pain covered his face.

They didn't seem particularly close, and I wasn't the best person to ask when it came to family matters, but being what he was, I knew that looks could be deceiving.

The Prince stood suddenly, not looking back once as he turned and left the room. The door shut softly behind him, and Xavier turned to me while Merrick looked at the Prince's now empty chair.

"Is there nothing you can do?" The knight's voice was soft as he asked the question.

But he already knew the answer.

"No, curses and hexes aren't my strong suit," my eyes looked blankly down at the table as I tried to think about what I could do. "A strong enough witch may be able to do something, but I don't know who you would be able to trust. With everything that's been going on, I'm not sure I would allow anyone from this kingdom to go near the king."

"I'm not sure I know anyone that would be helpful either," Merrick said, and being a mage, he would have better contacts.

"Then what do we do?" Xavier asked, running a hand through his hair in frustration. "We can't just let him die. He may not be the best king, not anymore, but that doesn't mean he deserves to die this way. Can we do nothing to help him?"

The only thing I could think of was ending his life, a sentiment that I didn't think would be appreciated right then. So instead of saying anything, I gathered the papers together into a pile in silence.

"Handle it how you see fit," I told them as I stood, pulling my hood over my face so that they wouldn't see the way my next words were going to affect me. "I don't care what happens to any of you. I've done all I'm obligated to, and I have nothing left to offer you."

Merrick looked at me sharply, though I didn't see a trace of anger on his face. Xavier just looked puzzled by my words, and West sent me a lazy smile as he watched me.

"Tell Maribelle that I appreciate everything, but I don't want to hear from any of you again," I said, turning to leave through the same door as the Prince.

"Don't worry," West called out, and I paused for a moment before continuing, his final words ringing through my ears as I shut the door behind me. "I'll take care of your guys until you come back for them."

CHAPTER NINETEEN

I GRUNTED WITH EFFORT AS I TOOK the last guy down, wiping the sweat and blood from my face with the inside of my cloak. One month of work left it as dirty as I was, but I couldn't seem to stop long enough to rest.

Anger and helplessness were pushing me on. I was on a mission to destroy the guild, and I was starting by hunting all the assassins down one by one. Or, four by four, as was the case with this group. The teams were getting better the more people I killed, and I had to wonder if the Guild Master was troubled by the large number of assassins that weren't coming back.

There was no doubt in my mind that he knew who was responsible for their deaths, but I also knew that he wouldn't go far outside the guild's walls himself. It wasn't that he couldn't, just that inside the boundary he was more powerful. He had created a magic bond with the building and the land, so it was like a continuous loop of power that would feed him while inside.

That just meant that I would have a bit of time to make a

plan before going after him. The downside was that he was able to prepare for me while also having the added benefit of more power at his disposal.

His main ability was that of a puppet master. He was able to control people and make them do his bidding with only a glance. The ability was much stronger than that of any of his son's, and the effects took years of being out of his presence to wear off completely. Something that he tried to avoid letting happen.

Sheer willpower was enough to block the effects, and I was able to fight his control, but I knew that if he put his full power, and the power he got from his surroundings, behind it, even I would fall victim to his abilities. It meant I would need to try and find a way to surprise him. If he didn't see me coming, he wouldn't have the time to stop me.

It was a long shot, but I would have to make it work. Or, I would need a way to block his power completely if I wanted to have a chance against him. On top of his abilities, he was the leader of the guild for a reason. He was fighter, and he was the one that had taught me almost everything I knew. A master of his abilities, both physical, and magical. A threat I wasn't sure I would be able to beat without luck on my side.

"Long time no see," West said as he walked out of the forest, his gaze taking in the three bodies before I lifted a hand and burned them to ash.

"And, to what do I owe this displeasure?" I asked, keeping my tone empty.

My eyes ran over his frame, and I was surprised to see that the cloak he was wearing had two emblems embroidered on it. One that was easily recognizable as the kingdom's flag. The dragon curled up and placed on a purple background, but I didn't recognize the second one.

He spoke before I could make out what it was, and I looked

up at him, following him with my gaze as he slowly started to circle me.

"Those are harsh words when I know that you've missed me terribly," he said with a smirk, his eyes watchful. "I'm here to make sure that you're okay. We hadn't heard from you in a while, and I was worried."

"Sure," I said, not believing him.

Though West was many things, a liar wasn't one of them. What he was saying was true in a sense, but like I was prone to doing, I was sure it was only a half-truth. There was another reason he was here.

"And," he said, finally stopping his circling to try and look at my face from under my hood. "We want you to come back to the castle."

"Ah..." I said, letting my voice trail off.

"The King isn't going to last much longer, and there's been more unrest that usual. The Prince wants to have someone he trusts at his back, and you're the only person that isn't known to those outside the castle. He needs someone that others wouldn't assume is with him. Someone he can trust."

West's voice was earnest, and I had to admit that my heart seemed to squeeze, but I had my own mission to accomplish. And this one was more important to me at the moment. As cold as it may have seemed, I was sure that the Guild Master had a hand in what was happening within the kingdom, and though I didn't see what he would get out of dethroning the Prince, I was sure he had been offered something too good for him to pass up.

With everything I had learned, and what I had seen, it was the only thing that made sense.

"I'm sorry, West," and I honestly *was* sorry. "But, I can't help you."

Despite what I had said when I walked out on them all those weeks ago, I hadn't meant to stay away for as long as I had. This was taking far longer than it should. The assassins were getting better at hiding and doing their jobs, and their actions almost seemed erratic. Between that and the missions I had been interfering with, I was sure that the Guild Master was plotting with whoever was in charge of this coup d'état.

The details of how they were planning to take the throne were still fuzzy, but I had a feeling they were going to try and use The Challenge for the crown. That meant I needed to try and stop it before that could happen.

There was no doubt that if they were able to get that far, they already had something planned to ensure that the Prince and his trusted friends would have trouble completing the trials. He would need to be more careful than ever if that were to happen.

I was close to being able to go after the Guild Master himself without the fear of having to fight the members at the same time. There was only thirteen left, and I knew where four of them were right now. The other nine were scattered to the wind, but rumor had it that three of them had turned their back on the Guild Master, and that only left six for me to deal with.

There was a part of me that wanted to deal with the Guild Master first, then go out to take care of them. But I wasn't sure if that would be better or worse, and in the end, I was going to have a hard-enough time dealing with the Guild Master without the threat of him having allies there to help him.

"That's what I thought you were going to say," West sighed, lowering his head to look at the ground.

"Then, why bother showing up at all?" I asked, weary all of a sudden. "What was the point in searching for me if you knew I wasn't going to come back with you?"

"Because they couldn't seem to find you on their own, and

we wanted to make sure you were alright," West said, a presence finally showing up on my radar just as the warmth from a male body seemed to heat up my back.

His circling me finally made sense, he had wanted to get my back to the Prince and friends, and I had fallen for it.

Adair wrapped his arm around me, resting it against my collar bone as he pulled me into his chest. A growl seemed to come from his throat, the sound soft as he bent his head to press it to the top of my own. His warmth seeped through the fabric of my hood and radiated throughout my body.

The familiarity, and the intimacy of the action surprised me, and my hands reached up to grab his arms, neither pulling him closer nor pushing him away, just resting on top of his skin.

"Stubborn Kitten," The Prince whispered in a voice much more gravely than I had heard before.

My lips tightened, and I wasn't sure what I was supposed to say. But I was too in shock to form words, anyway.

"Is there nothing we can say to convince you to come with us?" Xavier said, standing far too close to my left side, while Merrick moved to block my right.

When West stepped up to form a box around me, I wasn't sure if I should surrender, or if my fight or flight reflexes were going to kick in and I would end up taking them all out. My body didn't know how to react to being in such a vulnerable position among such powerful men.

Instinct said I could trust them, the bond as strong as ever. But I was an assassin, I knew better than to trust something as flimsy as emotion.

These were some of the most powerful men I had ever met, and I was trapped between them. At their mercy, and I knew it. Though, I still wasn't scared. It was the one emotion I never seemed to experience when they were around. At least, I didn't fear for my *own* safety.

My head dipped forward, resting on the Prince's arm as I tried to figure out what to do.

"You're a long way from the castle, Adair." My voice was soft and slightly mumbled as I spoke.

"Not as far as you might think," he said, and I knew he was talking about the fact that he would be able to cross the distance quickly, and not that it wasn't a long way away.

"I guess not," I said, just as quiet as the first time I had spoken.

"Ionia?" Merrick asked softly, and I had to release the Prince and clench my fists, digging my nails into my palms in an effort to remember my reasons for not going with them.

Then I realized that them coming here was all I needed to find that resolution. They were the reason I was out here in the first place. Them, and the other innocent and good people in the kingdom. Selfishly, they were my first priority, and I still wasn't sure why I had latched onto them so quickly, but I wasn't going to fight it.

"You guys shouldn't have come," I said, though I was happy to see them, even if I couldn't say the words.

"Sure," Xavier said, a smile on his face. "We're glad to see you too."

I chuckled, all the fight leaving me.

"Idiots," I said, the Prince finally releasing me and stepping back.

"Yep," West said, no apology in his voice.

"At least you're man enough to admit it," I said with a laugh.

He just smiled at me. Xavier threw an arm around my

shoulder, pulling me into his side. I let out a surprised noise as I fell into him. He tugged my hood down and surprised me even more when he pressed a kiss to the top of my head.

"What was that for?" I asked, trying my hardest not to blush.

"Because I wanted to do it," he said with a shrug.

I smiled, intending to say something, but just as I opened my mouth a familiar feeling ran through me.

"Ionia!" The voice belonged to Maribelle, and I knew without a shadow of a doubt that I wasn't going to get to her in time.

"No," I said, my voice breathless.

My magic surged and tried to take over, and I realized with a start that she was much closer than I expected, but I could tell by the weakness in her voice, that she didn't have long, and fear crept through me.

"Ion—" My body wouldn't let me stay standing.

Whether I wanted it or not, whether I was going to make it or not, Maribelle was calling me to her side, and I knew it was a trap even as I could feel it starting to close in on me.

Just like before, I felt my magic urge me to go faster than my physical body should have been capable of. But magic didn't care, my *promise* didn't care. Purple magic surrounded me, and I shook Xavier off as I started to run.

The forest was blurring past me so fast that it was only instinct and practice that kept me from crashing into the trees around me as I weaved through them. My connection to the earth allowing me to dodge the roots and other things that would try to trip me. My thighs burned and my breaths sawed in and out of my lungs.

A scream escaped when blinding pain exploded through me and my body pushed on even faster than before. Tears pressed behind my eyes at the pressure in my body and head.

Maribelle's life force was flickering, even as I got closer. Four other presences seeming to press in on me from behind.

I skidded to a stop in a clearing, my body reacting before I could even take stock of the situation. The man lost his head before he could even realize I had arrived, two others falling prey to my blades before the last three saw me and were able to fight back.

My magic pressed on me, and my body, still not completely my own at the moment, turned and ran to Maribelle.

She was nothing more than a pile of skin and bones, so torn up that I almost didn't recognize her.

"Sweety," I said softly, lightly brushing a hand over her face.

I used magic to make my touch feel soothing instead of painful like I knew it would be. She whimpered softly, and after a moment, I realized she was trying to talk to me.

"Sorry...tried...not to call...you..."

I gave her a soft smile, as I ran my hand once more over her face. Someone was standing over me, and despite the fact that I knew he was a threat, I couldn't force myself to turn. Maribelle was dying, and my magic demanded that I pay the price for not getting here fast enough to save her. Demanded that I make her feel better, even as she was slowly fading from this world.

The man above me let out a gurgle of surprised pain, then his body was thrown to the side, a supped-up Xavier standing in his place as I was forced to watch the life fade from my one female friend.

"You don't feel any pain, or fear," I told her, my voice taking on the musical quality associated with my ability. "You aren't scared, and you aren't alone."

Maribelle smiled, the sight terrifying instead of reassuring, and something inside me broke. Magic was gathering in my chest, compressing around my heart as it threatened to stop completely.

I couldn't breathe as I watched her eyes start to flutter shut, blood pooling around me and soaking my clothes worse when I pulled her onto my lap. Still, that macabre smile never left her face, even as I felt the warmth leave her body.

Something inside me shattered as she died, my magic taking out its price on my now splintered soul. All my muscles seized at once, my body stiffening and a groan releasing as wave after wave of pain flooded all my nerve endings, acid running through me and burning me from the inside out.

"What's happening to her?" West said, keeping his distance as Maribelle's body fell from my now limp arms.

"The cost of losing a life under her protection," Merrick said, his voice horrified. "She made a promise and bound it in magic, so now she has to pay the price for failing to save Maribelle's life."

"Yes, and it played out much better than I could have hoped," a new voice spoke up.

My body stopped seizing all at once, though the pain didn't. Suddenly his plan made sense, the sound of a cage slamming shut rang through my head.

"Jyria," I heard West whisper with both confusion and fear.

Even the light wielder was scared of the man, and that was saying something.

"This is the leader of the guild?" The Prince asked like he was looking for a fight.

I wanted to warn him, to tell him to leave, but I couldn't. I couldn't say anything.

"And you're the Prince that turned my most gifted assassin

against me," Jyria said with humor. "Now that introductions are complete, I think it's time for us to leave."

Just as the Guild Master started to turn, and the men looked like they were preparing to fight. My body moved without my permission, unable to protest or make a sound.

"Ah ah, I wouldn't do that if I were you," he smiled back at the men, a sick satisfaction on his face. "You won't like what happens if you try to attack me."

"And why is that?" Xavier said, his body bigger and more muscular than normal. "You're the one that should be scared."

"My intel told me that you cared for her," Jyria said before turning to meet my gaze. "I guess we were wrong."

The blade at my throat dug deeper, my own hand holding the weapon that was about to be the means of my death.

"Not one more step," The Guild Master said, making me press the blade deep enough that I drew blood.

The warmth flowed down my throat and left a stinging sensation behind, even as the blade froze where it was. I was trying to fight his control with everything inside of me, but it was barely making a dent in his power.

Adair stopped his forward movement, his gaze on mine before it flicked down to the knife in my hand.

"You're fast, Prince, I'll give you that. Not many people can keep up with a fae that's being pulled to a promise kissed. I would have loved to see what you were capable of," he said, then the tension in the air shifted, and I begged the Prince to run with my eyes while he could. "As a matter of fact..."

His words trailed off, but once again my body acted without my consent. Another weapon was in my hand, this time a long handled wooden staff with a blade on the end, it looked similar to a spear, but the blade was bigger.

The Prince was barely able to dodge the blow, my reach extended with the weapon, and my speed enhanced by my magic as it was forced to work against me the same way my body was.

"Kitten?" He asked softly, the others stepping back as I continued to move.

I turned, thrust, swung, and kept aiming to kill the Prince. My weapons were continuously switching as well, and though he made it look effortless, I could tell the Prince was just barely able to dodge my blows. He was starting to sweat, but he wasn't fighting back.

"Kitten, please," he said. "I know you can fight his control. You were able to fight off that man, Brand, before, right? And the other one, Barth? You can fight this man's control, too."

Unable to completely dodge my blow this time, a long, thin cut opened up on the Prince's chest, not deep enough to cause any lasting damage, but the sight of his blood was enough to make me hesitate.

My body paused just long enough that I saw hope enter the Prince's eyes.

"Run," I forced the word out, fighting the Guild Masters control so hard that it was causing me physical pain. "You need to *run*."

Because, while I was attacking him with a weapon, I was nowhere near completely under the Guild Master's control. He was forcing me to fight the Prince, but he couldn't control my magic, not yet.

"How sweet, she wants to save your life." The Guild Master taunted. "I would listen to her young man; she's doing everything she can not to kill you. But eventually she will be fully under my control. Then she won't be able to fight me off at all."

"You don't have complete control?" Merrick asked, horrified as he watched me start to attack the Prince again.

"No," West snorted, but the sound wasn't one of humor. "She's much too powerful to fall to him completely, but that doesn't mean she has control of her physical body."

"Eventually her mind and magic will be mine, but the traitor is right," Jyria sounded calm considering the conversation, knowing he didn't have full control of me. "But I've been working on her since she was a child, it shouldn't take too much longer before I'm able to override her will completely."

"Just how powerful is this fool?" Xavier said, looking between me and the Guild Master.

"Would you like to find out?" Jyria taunted him again.

Fear rose up inside me, and I pulled and threw a blade, the sharpened gemstone glinting in the light as the Guild Master was forced to dodge it. His glare moved to me, but I had successfully diverted his attention from the knight, and that was okay.

"Insolent brat," he snarled.

I grabbed my own wrist, quickly twisting and letting out a cry as I broke it with one swift movement. The guys let out calls of surprise, but the Guild Master didn't stop there. I drew one of my own blades, shoving it into my thigh even as the pain from fighting his control spread throughout my body.

"Ionia!" Adair snarled, but I couldn't stop when I didn't control my own actions.

"You're boring me," Jyria said as I fell to one knee, panting and still holding the blade inside my leg. "I think it's time we left."

"No," Adair said. "Please, take me instead."

The Prince stepped toward the Guild Master, and I wanted to

snarl at the idiot for saying something so stupid. Thankfully, I didn't have to.

Jyria started to laugh, forcing me to pull the blade from my leg and stand up like I hadn't just injured myself.

"I don't want you, Prince, but that was cute. You're going to get what's coming to you soon enough. Besides," the Guild Master said, his tone sharpening. "I could have brought you under my control anytime I wanted to."

Something about his words rang false, and my eyes widened the slightest bit. My gaze flicked to West, the only one looking at me instead of the Guild Master, and I saw when he recognized that I had just sensed the Guild Master's lie. He gave me an almost imperceptible nod.

"Liar," West called out, turning towards the Guild Master with a smirk firmly in place. "You can't control him any more than I could. The only person here that had a chance at getting him to listen to their orders is the woman you're threatening to kill."

The Guild Master clenched his jaw but said nothing. He wouldn't try and use me to order the Prince around. He may be able to stop me from speaking to a point, but he couldn't control my words, not yet.

As I was staring at the Guild Master, my vision started to flicker, once again causing the world's color to fade in and out. The Guild Master's color was a dark brown, and almost seemed to darken in spots. Focusing, I forced the grey world to stay, focusing on that instead of the eye that still saw color, and what I saw surprised me.

I had done some experimenting over the last month, and while I wasn't able to control when my eye flickered, I could control it a bit when it happened. I had realized that what I was seeing was a mix between people's auras, soul, and magic. The combination was still hard for me to pick apart, but this was the first time I had seen something that was a manifestation of a physical ailment.

The Guild Master was sick, and extremely sick at that. Illness was eating up his body from the inside, and sooner or later he would start to fall weaker. He wouldn't be able to keep control of me for long. He would never gain full control of me, and in fact, he was going to die long before that happened.

A smile crossed my face, and the world's colors slowly came back into focus.

"What are you smirking at?" The Guild Master snarled at me.

I realized all at once that he hadn't yet realized he was ill. He didn't know that he was going to die soon.

My smile widened, and I heard the others start to murmur to each other.

"Kitten?" The Prince asked, taking a cautious step forward.

The dagger I had just rammed into my leg rose to press against my throat, but my smile still didn't fade, even when the Guild Master made me press hard enough to draw more blood.

"Tell me what you're smiling about, or I will force these men to watch as I slowly make you kill yourself."

"One day soon, Guild Master, you are going to regret what you've done here today. You are going to regret that you brought me under your control, and I'm going to watch as you die a slow and painful death."

My voice was calm and rang with truth. The Guild Master almost seemed to pause as he thought over my words.

"You're sure?" West asked, not questioning me as much as trying to reassure himself that I wasn't lying.

"I'm going to enjoy watching you suffer," I said, the cold broken part of my soul shining through in that moment, the words I had spoken not a lie in the least.

"Kitten?" Adair said, his voice concerned.

He knew what I was about to do, knew I was going to go with the Guild Master, and I knew he wouldn't understand why.

I was going to be dealt extreme amounts of pain before the Guild Master finally fell to his illness, but I also knew that this would give me the chance to ensure he died. I would do what I could to make it happen faster. But in order to do that I would need to go with him now. I would allow him to hurt me, knowing that I would be the victor in the end.

"Leave us," I said, the words coming out as an order, though I didn't compel them to listen.

It was as much a request as a test of just how much West's words from before were correct. I didn't believe for one moment that I held some sway over the Prince, but I figured he would listen if I had reason. And I had a very good reason.

"Leave me," I said again, meeting Adair's gaze.

After a moment of enduring the Prince's searching eyes, he nodded. I switched my gaze to the others, getting all of them to nod their agreement one at a time. Though none of them looked happy about it.

"We'll see you soon, Kitten." The Prince said, his tone warning me that it wasn't a question.

"If you don't show up, we're going to come for you," Xavier said, his body slowly returning to normal.

The others nodded at that, all of them watching me as I nodded my agreement.

"You'll be too busy trying to save yourselves to worry about her," the Guild Master snorted.

"I'll see you soon," I told them, ignoring the Guild Master completely.

It would be a little longer than they probably suspected, but I *would* see them again.

"Stay safe, Kitten," the Prince said, then he turned, leading the others out of the clearing, and out of my life.

At least, for the moment.

"They really are quite dull witted, aren't they?" The Guild Master said, thinking he had won.

I didn't say anything, just turned to follow him as he forced me to walk beside him, my thigh still burning, each step a reminder of what I was about to do. Who I was trying to protect.

I would see them soon enough, I just hoped that they were able to stay safe until I made it back to them.

CHAPTER TWENTY

TIME WAS PASSING SLOWLY, AND YET, it felt like everything had happened in the blink of an eye.

Bars surrounded me and the warmth was seeping from me and into the cold floor. Much like my life blood as I was once again forced to slowly dig my own dagger into my stomach. It was the fourth time he had made me perform this move in the last hour, and it hadn't gotten any easier to deal with the pain.

The room wasn't large, but the sound of my pained breaths seemed to be the only sound as they echoed back to me.

"Give up already, girl," Jyria snarled.

"No," I panted.

It was almost time. I was almost strong enough to fight him off.

His illness had wreaked havoc through his system, and I knew that he was starting to feel its effects. His skin was pale and sweaty. The pain he was feeling coming more and more often until it was almost constant.

But he had stepped up his own game recently, as well. Four months of torture at my own hands had driven me to the brink of insanity many times. Every time I had come close to falling over that ledge, I heard a voice, a male voice, whispering my name.

"*You're going to be okay; you have to be.*"

"*Don't let him win, Ionia.*"

"*Come on, Guild Master, hurry up and deal with him already.*"

"*See you soon, Kitten.*"

The voice was different every time, but all of them were familiar. And it always pulled me away from the call of insanity.

The Guild Master growled. Then, without saying anything, he turned and walked away from the cage that I was being kept in. It was an iron contraption, and he had been surprised to find out that I didn't share the same allergy as the rest of my people, but I also hadn't been able to escape.

Though, I hadn't really tried too hard.

A few hours later, I felt it. It was like a shock blast throughout the kingdom, the death of the King sending out a wave of magic telling the people that it was time to morn.

My heart broke, not because I cared for the king, but because I wasn't there to be with the Prince when his father passed.

As soon as the magic swept over me, it seemed to stop, and surprise filled me when instead of passing through, it gathered inside me.

The king's magic was lending me it's strength to fight my way free. His will allowing me to finish what I had set out to accomplish all those months ago. My healing kicked into overdrive, not healing me completely, but enough that I was able to move without risking death.

I stood and moved over to the gate, putting pressure on the areas that I knew would give me the leverage needed to open it without the key. It took more strength than I had at the moment, but I muscled through the pain, and forced my body to push harder.

With a loud squeal it finally released, and it jerked to the side with a slam. The noise was loud, and I heard the sound of the Guild Master coming towards me. Fear slammed into me, not able to stop it even though I was finally planning to kill the man.

He came into view as I stepped over the threshold of the cage, his gaze taking in the messed-up door, and the fact that I was now standing outside of the iron bars.

I could feel him trying to control me, trying to force me back into the cage, but the king's magic rose up, stopping him from being able to get a hold of my will. I wasn't sure what had caused the king's magic to assist me, but I knew that it was the only thing that was allowing me to keep control of my senses.

"How are you doing that?" The Guild Master asked, panting with the effort he was using.

I didn't answer his question, and instead stepped closer to the man.

He was way too weak to put up much of a fight, and a part of me was sad to see someone who had once been so powerful fall so low. He had been like a father to me once, and I didn't think that feeling would ever fade completely, but he had tried to have me killed. He had tried to have the Prince and the others killed.

"I hope you find peace," I told him, stepping close and ramming my blade into his throat before he could make a move to counter my actions.

Instead of a snarl, a smile spread across his face as the life faded from his eyes.

A wave of magic escaped him, similar to the kings, but I knew that it wouldn't go farther than the area the Guild Master had ruled over. The ending of a cycle of magic.

His body fell to the floor at my feet, and I stared at him for a moment as I felt the king's magic leave my body as suddenly as it had come.

I grunted as pain washed over me, all my strength leaving at once now that I had accomplished what I had wanted to. I forced my body to stumble down the hallway, barely making it to my old room in time to collapse on the bed I used to call my own.

My eyes closed as exhaustion and weariness overwhelmed my senses, a healing sleep stealing over me. I would be dead to the world for the next few hours at least, I only hoped nothing big happened before I could get back to the Prince.

Though I had a feeling that things were only going to get worse from here on out. Something was coming, not just the coup, but something else was hanging over our heads, and I needed to get back to them as soon as possible to stop it. I just had to.

ADAIR'S POV

The medical room was lit by only a few candles as I sat next to the large bed.

"I'm sorry, My Prince," one of the women said as she placed a hand on my shoulder.

It made my skin crawl; the only female touch my creature

wanted was one I wouldn't be feeling anytime soon. I shook those thoughts away, trying to work through the pain that was growing in my chest.

I sat at my father's side as he breathed his last, knowing that, even as I mourned, there was work to be done.

My kitten and West were right, and the situation that I found myself in now was a tricky one.

Xavier limped into view; his body as bruised as his ego. Two days ago, he had been caught up in a spell that had done its best to kill him. Thankfully, he was stronger than the wizards had thought, and all it had done was cause him to be temporarily out of a job.

Merrick on the other hand...

I looked over at the bed my other best friend was currently occupying. West on the bed beside him. None of them were in good enough shape to face the danger I could feel coming. My own body had taken a beating, but my creatures soul sped up my recovery to the point that I wouldn't be injured for much longer.

Even knowing that it was dangerous, I couldn't help but wish my kitten was here with us now. I had a feeling that none of this would have happened if she had been here. She had a way of turning the odds in her favor, even when they shouldn't be, and it wasn't something she wasn't even aware of.

"She'll come back," West muttered to himself.

He was as worried as the rest of us when it came to how long our kitten was taking to claw her way back to us.

We had all felt it over the past couple of months, the fact that she was on the brink of something horrible. It was almost like she was reaching out to us for help, but we weren't sure how to reach her back.

A few words of reassurance, and she was gone, the feeling of clarity emanating from her as her presence faded once again.

It was frustrating to say the least, knowing that she was so close, and yet so far from my side. I knew my brothers understood the feeling. All of us were attached to the small woman.

"She will," I agreed, even though I knew he wasn't speaking to me.

"Your Highness," one of the younger knights ran into the room, panting. "There are men gathering in the courtyard outside, and they are demanding to see you."

I sighed, looking down at my father sadly. The man had been great once, but recently, I had seen something inside him change. It was around the same time that he had started to get sick. The two must have been related, because the man that had raised me would never have acted the way my father had at the end. Still, I loved him fiercely, and now he was gone, his body not even cooled before our newest threat was pounding on the castle doors.

"I see," I said, standing despite the way my body protested the movement.

The young man looked at all the pathetic souls filling the infirmary, Xavier trying and failing to walk towards us.

"You're to stay here," I demanded, and I saw something mutinous cross his face. "I need you to heal as fast as you can. We both know our visitors don't come in peace, but I can put them off for a few days, at least. So, for now, rest and prepare yourself."

With a disgruntled expression he nodded, moving to rest back on the bed he had stood up from. A sigh of relief escaping him, and forcing a chuckle from me despite the situation we were in.

Shaking my head, I made my way into the hall, all the people bowing their heads to me as I passed them. There were more than a few faces that were covered in tears, and I knew I wasn't the only one that would miss my father. Clenching my fists, I forced myself to push past the sorrow and focus on the here and now. There would be time to mourn later; for now, I had to make sure that the castle and my people were safe.

It wouldn't do to have my kitten come back into an unsafe situation. She was facing her own demons; she didn't need to come back and deal with mine, too.

Two men stood beside the doors, pulling them open as I arrived, allowing me to walk out and make a dramatic entrance that would usually make me roll my eyes.

The crowd gathered outside was large, and some of my people from the town below were also gathered, wringing their hands with fear. They knew something wasn't right with the large group gathered before me. As far as I could tell with my brief glance, there were six distinct groupings, two from the neighboring kingdom.

"What is the meaning of this?" I roared across the crowd allowing my creature to add his power to the demanded question.

"We've come to—" the man I recognized as the Fourth Prince of the other kingdom started, but I interrupted him, knowing that if I allowed him to finish, it would set things into motion too fast for me to stop.

"You dare come interfere in our time of mourning?" I growled, the sound spreading over those gathered, and causing a few to shiver with fear. "My father, the King of this realm, has just passed away. I am owed at least four days of peace to plan his funeral and make other arrangements. This was something that all kingdoms agreed to as one; are you telling me that you are breaking that treaty? Are you declaring war?"

I saw the other Prince's eyes widen, knowing that he was probably here without permission from his own father. If he continued with his plan now, he would be declaring war, and we would march on his kingdom, taking his own family by surprise as we demanded retribution for crimes they wouldn't have known he had committed.

Not to mention, his planning would have been made moot. He wouldn't have been able to demand anything of me if we were at war. Even if I never made a move on his own kingdom.

"No," he gritted out between clenched teeth, his fists so tight his fingers had gone white. "I've come to offer my sincerest condolences for your loss."

It was clear to all those that were gathered his words weren't sincere, but I didn't care. I had just bought us four days. Four days to figure out how to win an unknown battle when all my friends were injured. My eyes narrowed on one a few of the magic users in the crowd that had come with the men. Were they the one responsible for what had happened to my father? My friends?

It didn't matter now. I needed to figure out a way to get my friends and I healed, and how to keep them safe for the next four days. There was something about the confidence the young Prince had pranced into my courtyard wearing that made me think he was much better prepared for what was about to happen than I was. Like he knew something I didn't.

"Thank you for your concern," I said, my voice not anymore sincere than his had been.

He nodded, a smirk curling up the sides of his mouth.

"See you in four days, Prince Adair."

I didn't bother to respond as he turned and walked out of the inner gates, watching as the others followed. The people of my kingdom looked to me, and I nodded at them in reassurance.

There was no way I would allow my kingdom to fall into the hands of someone like him. I would figure out what his game was, then I would beat him at it.

I would win, for my friends, for my kitten, and for my people.

IONIA'S POV

I woke to the feeling of someone standing over me.

"Oh, thank god," the woman said, stepping back as I swung up into a sitting position, blade at the ready.

She lifted her hands, face covered in fear.

"I'm not here to hurt you," she said, and her face was familiar, though it took me a moment to figure out where I knew her from.

"Gwendolyn?" I asked, not lowering my blade, but instead raising it higher. "What are you doing here? Trying to plant another bomb?"

Her face paled, and I noticed that she was shaking like a leaf.

"I—you have to understand, they had my mother," she said, and her voice rang out with truth, making me lower my blade the slightest bit. "I didn't know what they were planning, only that I was supposed to cause a scene, and make sure that I put that thing on you."

"And I'm just supposed to believe you?" I asked her. "I'm not going to let you get close to the Prince. You're crazy if you think I'm going to allow you to harm him."

Her lips compressed, and her eyes filled with tears, but I didn't think it was my words that caused them.

"They lied," she said, confusing me with her words. "They said if I did what they asked, they would release my mother. But they didn't let her go, they killed her, then my father, right in front of me. They lied, and now I'm alone. Both my parents are gone, and it's all my fault."

She fell to her knees as sobs overtook her. I watched for a moment, waiting for her to make a move, but she didn't, her words and emotions were authentic. There didn't seem to be anything else at play here, and all the negative feelings had felt around her before were gone.

I sighed, then knelt down, putting my blade back where it belonged. Lifting my arm, I slowly wrapped it around her shoulder, not knowing how to offer comfort, but knowing that when the Prince or the other guys touched me it soothed something inside of me.

She stiffened at first, but soon leaned into me, crying into the dirty fabric of my underclothes. I had been stripped of my armor as soon as we arrived, so the shirt I was wearing was tattered and dirty, filled with sweat, blood, and my own tears as well as the debris of the floors I had laid upon.

Her sobs slowly turned to sniffles, and soon enough she started to calm down.

"Thank you," she said, her voice rougher than before. "Not to be mean, but...you kind of...smell..."

I looked at her, and the absurdity of the situation hit me, and it made me start laughing. As soon as I started, I couldn't seem to stop, and Gwendolyn stared at me in horror while I did so.

"Four months of torture will do that to you," I said as I continued laughing, her face only seeming to grow more horrified.

"What?" She whispered.

"Nothing," I said, whipping the tears of laughter that had escaped. "What are you doing here, Gwendolyn?"

"Gwen," she said. "Please, call me Gwen."

"Alright, Gwen," I agreed, not bothering to argue for the moment. "What made you brave coming into the assassin's guild?"

She took a deep breath, a new fear seeming to come to her face. "I need your help."

That made me pause. I was shocked that she had braved the house of assassins to ask for help from someone she had tried to kill.

"No, not me," she said, confusing me more as she seemed to struggle to find the words. "The Prince needs you. The Prince and his friends all need your help."

My gaze focused intently on her face, all my laughter gone. She seemed to shrink when I continued to look at her.

"What do you mean they need me? What happened to them? Are they all right?" My words were hard, and I could see that she feared that I would harm her if she didn't give me the answer I wanted to hear. "Don't lie to me, tell me what happened,"

I stood and started to rip the already tattered clothes from my body, ignoring the other girl in the room.

"They..." her words trailed off, and I turned, ready to demand answers only to find her looking at the scars and wounds covering my body with horror.

My expression softened when I looked at her next. It was one thing to hear that someone had been forced to endure pain, but it was another to see the scars that proved it. Not only that, but the girl had witnessed the death of her parents, my scars were probably a reminder of the wounds they had sustained.

"Gwen?" I said softly, her gaze raising to meet my own. "Please, tell me what's happening with my guys?"

The words slipped from my tongue, but if she noticed she didn't say anything. Instead, she seemed to gather herself. Something in her solidifying as she got to her own feet.

"Right," she said with a nod, going over to the wash basin in the corner and waving over the bowl.

I watched with amusement as the bowl filled with warm water, knowing I would have been able to do the same thing, but appreciating the gesture none the less.

This woman before me was much different than the one I had met months ago. She had changed drastically, and I had a feeling it was more than just witnessing her parents die that had done it.

"Thank you," I said.

Then, instead of using the rag, I waved my hand, watching as the water rose from the bowl, and guided it to run across my body, cleaning me as it went. It didn't take long before I was squeaky clean, but I was getting more and more anxious when Gwendolyn didn't speak.

"Gwen," I said, my voice exasperated.

She seemed to shake her head, bringing her thoughts back to the present.

"The King died yesterday," she said, and I nodded to let her know I was aware of that. "Minutes after that, a large group of men gathered in the courtyard in front of the castle. I don't know the exact details, but I know that they were getting ready to demand something before the Prince stopped them by demanding a mourning period."

I smiled at that. Clever Prince. A period of mourning was a

four-day period that demanded peace. It was something that all the kingdoms had agreed upon, and if any of the kingdoms broke this agreement, all the others would join up and crush them. It allowed for the royal family to mourn without fear, and also allowed them to get their affairs in order.

"The problem is, the Prince and his friends are in no condition to fight the men off. I know about the challenge for the crown, but while I was with the guys that were plotting against the Prince, I found out that the Prince himself can't fight in it, he has to have a champion to do so in his place."

"What?" I asked, a new horror taking over my mind.

"It's an old rule that hasn't been put into effect since the first challenge, but there also hasn't been a challenge for the crown set forth in so long I doubt anyone would remember this." She said, wringing her hands as she watched me get dressed, pulling out and packing the sets of armor I never thought I would wear. "And if that wasn't bad enough, all the Prince's friends, as well as all the people that are strong enough to fight in his stead, have been severely injured."

My eyes flicked up to meet hers, my magic seeming to pulse with my heartbeat as I took in the meaning of her words.

"They're hurt?" I asked her softly.

"None of them will die, though it was a near thing. But none of them are in fighting condition either, and they won't be able to step in when the challenge it issued in three days."

That meant I had been out for at least a day since the death of the king, and it I was finally seeing why she had come here. I appreciated her actions, but I was wary of them, too.

"And you came to me, but what do you get out of this? I'm assuming you want something."

She bit her lip, nerves taking her over. Yet, despite the fact I knew she wanted something, I still wasn't getting any sinister vibes from her.

"I wanted to ask for a pardon for my actions from before, and a chance to prove that I've changed. I wanted to ask to be allowed to stay inside this kingdom, even if I have to fight to earn everything I can. I'll do it, just, please, help me stay."

I tilted my head as I looked her over. It wasn't just her personality that had changed, the feel of her magic had changed as well. My vision flickered, and I was surprised, firstly, because I had called it to me this time, and secondly because of what I saw.

Her intentions were pure, she really was trying to change. There were a few dark spots, but they were almost transparent, like they hadn't ever fully formed. But they were starting to fade away as well.

"Alright," I said, surprising us both. "I'll help you, but you have to prove what you said was true. You need to prove that you've changed. When we take back the crown for Adair, I will ask him to pardon your crimes, but if you willingly turn on us at any point, I will kill you myself. Are we clear?"

Despite the fact that I had just threatened her life, a smile took over her face, more tears starting to gather behind her eyes.

"Yes, we're clear," she said, nodding so fast I was worried she would damage her brain.

Sticking out my hand, she grabbed it without hesitation to shake.

"A deal is struck," I said, magic coursing through both of us as we were bound in a magical agreement.

She gasped, her eyes going wide. But there still wasn't fear in her gaze, just surprise.

"Then let's go save my Prince," I said.

"Right," she agreed, nodding again.

Strapping on the last of my weapons, I looked her over, figuring out the fastest way to get to the castle on foot.

"How do you feel about sharing your magic?"

She looked at me for a moment, and I couldn't help but smile at her confusion.

"Sure...?"

"Great," I said. "Then get ready to hold on tight, and you'll probably want to keep your eyes shut."

Worry filled her gaze, but she followed me when I started to lead her out of the room.

"Don't worry," I told her with a chuckle. "I won't drop you."

I heard her swallow, but she still didn't say anything.

I'm   coming   Prince,   just   you   wait.

CHAPTER TWENTY-ONE

ADAIR'S POV

IT HAD BEEN FOUR DAYS, AND WE STILL weren't any better. If anything, Xavier and the others were *worse*. I had been going out of my mind trying to help them while I tried to figure out a way to stop the other Prince's plans.

I hadn't been able to come up with anything useful.

There was nothing recorded on how to stop a challenge. In fact, all the books about the challenges had mysteriously disappeared, along with one of the newest knight recruits.

It wasn't hard to figure out what had happened, but now I was left with three ailing friends, and no way to stop the challenge for the throne.

"They're here," the same young knight from before said as he entered the room.

I nodded, forcing myself to my feet as my three companions did the same. I wasn't going to tell them not to come; they wouldn't listen if I did. My right to the crown was about to be challenged, and I was going to have to fight for the right to rule the people I had grown up getting to know.

Years of sweat, blood, and effort had made it so that I could improve the kingdom once I took my father's place. I had spent time with those in my kingdom, from the poor to the rich, I had learned all about their stations, helping those I could, and protecting those that needed it. Now, that was about to be thrown up into the air, a challenge set forth that would put those I cared about at risk.

The creature inside me stirred, its desire to protect our people, our treasures, making him want to come forward. I held him back, knowing that now wasn't the time.

"We're coming," I told him, slowing my pace to match that of my friends, and receiving a glare in response.

"I wish Ionia was here; she would have found a way to stop this from happening," Xavier said wistfully.

While I agreed, there was a part of me that hoped she was somewhere safe, away from all of this.

West snorted, in the best shape out of the three of them. "She would have killed them all before they ever reached the kingdom. No one would have ever known what was happening, and the bodies never would have been found."

It was a crude yet accurate statement, and I couldn't help the smile it brought to my face.

"Our kitten sure does have a way of using those claws of hers," I agreed, and it was a thought that made my inner beast almost seem to purr.

All of them smiled at the thought of how Ionia used her sparkling blades. The image of her grabbing the troll's axe in the fight in the garden came to mind. She had stopped it with pure, brute strength, and then leapt delicately onto his weapon, using her speed and skill to take his life before he even had a chance to attack her again, saving my men at the same time.

My happy thoughts faded as we approached the door leading to courtyard, knowing that what was about to happen would change the fate of the kingdom.

The doors were pulled open, the two men bowing their heads in respect as we passed, not able to hide their fear. It wasn't a secret, the fact that there was going to be a challenge, and by the number of people gathered outside, I knew that it had already spread throughout the main city. The whole of the kingdom probably knew by now.

We all stopped on the landing at the top of the stairs to look down on those that were about to oppose us, my best friends at my back. Though, I couldn't help but feel that someone was missing. I knew who it was. And so did the others.

"Hello, Fourth Prince Leonard of Wixley," I said, intentionally using the *fourth* in his title.

His face twisted, bitter that he was fourth in line to his own throne. Greed for the title of King was what had driven him here in the first place, and I was going to rub it in his face as much as I could.

"Prince Adair," he said, his tone almost a growl.

It wasn't very intimidating, poor human.

"You know why I'm here," he said, puffing his chest up like a bird that was getting ready to dance for a potential mate.

"Yes," I agreed calmly, enjoying the look of annoyance that crossed his face when I didn't say more.

"I, Prince Leonard—"

"Fourth Prince," I interrupted him.

He gritted his teeth and continued like he hadn't heard me.

"—Challenge you, with the approval of your council, to the right to take over the throne and stand as the new king of Dragon's Vale."

The silence after his challenge was deafening, and the smug smirk never left his face.

"And we are here to join the challenge that has been put forth," the five other leaders of the group I had noticed before stepped up.

One other man aside from Leonard was from his kingdom, but the other four were lords from my own lands. My eyes took in their faces, burning them into my memory in case they survived this challenge. I would kill them all for attempting to take from me what was rightfully mine.

"I accept your challenge," I said, murmurs starting throughout the crowd.

It wasn't like I had a choice of whether or not I accepted. The council had agreed for me, and all of them would be replaced as soon as I took back my crown.

A trickle of worry ran through me when the other Prince's smile widened instead of fading. He still had a trick up his sleeve, and I wasn't sure what it was. But I had a bad feeling that it was something that was about to shake my chances of winning a fight that I shouldn't have had to participate in in the first place.

"Great," the other Prince snarled.

He gestured behind him, and a wizard stepped forward, the power rolling off him in waves. His expression was cocky, and I did my best to hide my confusion at his reason for stepping up, forcing my face to stay blank.

"This is my chosen champion, as royalty isn't allowed to

fight in the actual competition. Of course, the other competitors are able to choose someone to stand in for them as well." He said smugly.

And there it was.

My fingers wanted to close around the dastardly man's throat at the realization that he had played me. And played me well.

There was no doubt that he was responsible for the misfortunes that had befallen my friends, but now he had taken away all three of the people I could have chosen to fight in my stead.

I watched as four of the lords also gestured their chosen champions forward, only one choosing to fight for himself. I looked them all over, wondering if there was a chance that any of my friends would survive against them in their current state.

Aside from the wizard that Leonard had brought, there was a shifter, a bear if his scent was an indication, then there was a vampire, also powerful in his own way. The third man was dressed in dark leathers, and when West sucked in a breath, I assumed he knew the man.

"Assassin," he whispered, quiet enough only I would hear.

So, we had a wizard, bear shifter, vampire, and witch assassin, by the feel of their magic. The fourth was part troll, but it seemed like he would have speed as well as strength on his side. The fifth man was the one that worried me the most aside from the wizard. He seemed to exude power, and the smell he was giving off made me think he was part shifter, and part magic user.

"Well, shit," Merrick breathed.

"Succinctly put," Xavier said with a pained chuckle.

"So, Prince Adair," Leonard said with a smirk. "Who will you choose to be your champion?"

All three of the men behind me tensed like they would volunteer, but I wouldn't let them kill themselves. Thinking quickly, I couldn't seem to find of a way out of this situation. The option of giving in was never really there, but now I was stuck between sacrificing one of my best friends or having to give over my crown to whomever won between the six men standing in front of us.

"Oh dear, it looks like none of your companions are in any shape to step up, are they?" Leonard taunted me. "Are you ready to concede yet?"

My mind was spinning, my anger growing with my helplessness as I realized that the people I had fought so hard to protect, and the people of my kingdom were all about to be handed over to the greedy idiots in front of me.

I wouldn't sacrifice my friends to this mad man. I would just have to bow out now, and figure something out later to get my crown back. Hopefully, it wouldn't take too long.

I opened my mouth, ready to bow out as gracefully as possible when another voice sent sparks racing throughout my body.

"Sorry I'm late, Prince, but my invitation seemed to have gotten lost in the mail."

My gaze rose to see a hooded figure sitting on the wall, leg up like she didn't have a care in the world.

Another woman stood beside her, shaking like a leaf, and it only took me a few seconds to recognize the face of Gwendolyn.

What was my kitten doing with the woman that tried to get her put to death? Never mind that, what was she doing here at all?

"Who are you?" Leonard said at the same time the man West had said was an assassin let out a curse.

"Oh shit," he said, looking at the Lord who was staring at him in surprise. "I'm out. I quit. Choose a different person to be your champion."

"You can't leave, you've signed a contract. A magical one, at that. If you bail now, you're as good as dead anyway." The Lord grumbled.

Leonard looked between my kitten and the other assassin with a calculating gaze before his eyes came back to me.

"Who is this? You can't just have anyone volunteer for the position," Leonard said, though I knew he didn't take the threat that Ionia presented seriously.

"Oh, I'm not just anybody," she said, scooping up Gwendolyn like she weighed nothing and leaping down off the wall in one move.

"I don't know who you are," the Fourth Prince said haughtily. "You haven't been in the castle in the past few months, so the Prince can't possibly know you. That means he doesn't trust you, and I doubt even he would be desperate enough to let just anybody fight for his crown."

"Your right," she said, moving through the crowd of people who parted for her without prompting. "He wouldn't let just anybody fight for his crown."

She made it up the stairs, placing a white-faced Gwendolyn on her feet beside Merrick with a meaning full look.

The young woman nodded before shakily putting her arm on Merrick's, looking like she was using it for support. Magic started to filter through the air at their contact, and the urge to rip her hand from my friend's arm was strong, but my kitten trusted her. So, for now, I would as well.

"Quit talking in circles and answer me!" Leonard demanded, getting upset that the attention wasn't all on him at the moment.

"My apologies, *Fourth* Prince Leonard," Ionia said snarkily, and I had to bite my tongue so I wouldn't laugh.

My kitten was here, and she was ready to fight. I had never been more relieved, or more scared for her in my life. But the guys were right earlier: she would have been able to help us fix everything, so while I didn't like the thought of her fighting in my place. She was our best chance at making sure the kingdom didn't fall into the wrong hands.

IONIA'S POV

While I still wasn't at one hundred percent, I was feeling much better now that I was here with the guys. Just being around them seemed to make all my aches and pains fade. At least, temporarily. The journey had taken longer than I wanted, and we almost didn't make it in time.

Despite the show the Fourth Prince was putting on, he wasn't as stupid as he appeared. Either that, or one of the other men that had stepped forward had wanted to ensure nothing happened to stop this from proceeding.

There had been people set up throughout the border of all the towns that I had needed to take care of before we could move forward. Thankfully, I had met up with a few of the other assassins on our side along the way.

Now that the time had come, they had given me the information that they had gathered and, still wanting to help, they had agreed to help me accomplish my goals to help the Prince save his kingdom.

While I didn't relish the thought of putting myself into the spotlight to fight, as soon as I had seen the state the men were in, I knew it was the only thing we could do. I was flying by the seat of my pants, and I didn't like the feeling of not being prepared.

I looked down at the six men that posed a threat to the kingdom and my Prince, taking in what my assassins were able to find out, and organizing the information in my head. All of them were dangerous in their own way, and I had no doubt that the challenges set forth would be designed for them to excel. It just meant I would need to be smarter, faster, and stronger than all of them.

Usually, I wasn't one to make a scene, but this man, this *arrogant* asshole of a man, needed to realize that he had messed with the wrong people. I only had to hope that it wouldn't backfire on me later.

"Report!" I called out, turning to face the crowed.

Four other assassins came out of the crowd, one jumping from the roof behind us.

"All threats taken care of, Guild Master," The man behind me said.

"Thank you," I said with a nod.

"It isn't kind, or smart, to try and kill the Prince in front of this many people," I stated, turning to face the man who had called the challenge. "Thankfully, we were able to save you from your own stupidity."

Leonard's face went angry for a moment before he seemed to gather himself.

"I don't know what you're talking about," he sniffed.

"Of course not," I said, the laughter in my voice clear.

"Kitten, what are you doing?" Adair asked me, stepping close enough his warmth seeped through my cloak.

"Waiting," I said.

"For what?" He asked softly, getting close enough his chest was almost touching my back.

"Oh, screw this," a man in the crowd said, stepping forward and raising a bow.

He released the arrow with a twang, and time seemed to slow as I watched it get closer, the trajectory of the weapon aiming for my heart. My arm moved on instinct, grabbing the shaft, and squeezing as the friction burned my palm before it stopped an inch from my chest.

"That," I said softly, gesturing to the man. "I knew we missed one, but I lost him in the crowd."

"I see," the Prince said, his voice dark.

I raised the arrow, showing him the tip gleaming with poison.

"Seems they really enjoy using poison," I told him, handing the arrow to Gwendolyn who reached a hand back and took it without looking.

I flicked my fingers and two of the assassins in the crowd grabbed the man, dragging him kicking and screaming past us into the castle. They would take him down to the cells where he would wait to be questioned.

"Who in the hell are you?" Leonard all but screamed, and for a moment I had forgotten he was there, forgotten the reason all of them were here.

"Oh, I apologize," I said, smiling under my hood. "My name is Ionia, Master of the Assassin's Guild, Friend of the Elements, and the Prince's personal bodyguard."

"Well shit," The bear shifter said, a smile on his face. "This competition just got more interesting."

And as I stood looking out at the men I was going to have to kill, I couldn't have agreed more.

Acknowledgment

I'd like to thank the fuzzy buttholes that share my abode. You sir's are adorable demons sent to stop me from finishing this book. But the joke is on you, because now it's published.

About the Author

Indra Frost is a fiction author who was born and raised in Utah where she currently resides. She has another day job, but hopes to eventually become a full-time author. When she's not writing she loves reading, food, and hanging out with family and friends.

She is also the author of A Gypsy's Magic - At World's End Anthology, and Candy's Confections - Cupid's Playthings Anthology, which are no longer in print. She plans to extend and re-publish both works on her own at a later date.

Also by Indra Frost

Ringleader's Revenge

Imps & Angels